HOMETOW

SHIPM

Stranger in Town by Brenda Novak
Baby's First Homecoming by Cathy McDavid
Her Surprise Hero by Abby Gaines
A Mother's Homecoming by Tanya Michaels
A Firefighter in the Family by Trish Milburn
Tempted by a Texan by Mindy Neff

SHIPMENT 2

It Takes a Family by Victoria Pade
The Sheriff of Heartbreak County by Kathleen Creighton
A Hometown Boy by Janice Kay Johnson
The Renegade Cowboy Returns by Tina Leonard
Unexpected Bride by Lisa Childs
Accidental Hero by Loralee Lillibridge

SHIPMENT 3

An Unlikely Mommy by Tanya Michaels
Single Dad Sheriff by Lisa Childs
In Protective Custody by Beth Cornelison
Cowboy to the Rescue by Trish Milburn
The Ranch She Left Behind by Kathleen O'Brien
Most Wanted Woman by Maggie Price
A Weaver Wedding by Allison Leigh

SHIPMENT 4

A Better Man by Emilie Rose
Daddy Protector by Jacqueline Diamond
The Road to Bayou Bridge by Liz Talley
Fully Engaged by Catherine Mann
The Cowboy's Secret Son by Trish Milburn
A Husband's Watch by Karen Templeton

SHIPMENT 5

His Best Friend's Baby by Molly O'Keefe
Caleb's Bride by Wendy Warren
Her Sister's Secret Life by Pamela Toth
Lori's Little Secret by Christine Rimmer
High-Stakes Bride by Fiona Brand
Hometown Honey by Kara Lennox

SHIPMENT 6

Reining in the Rancher by Karen Templeton
A Man to Rely On by Cindi Myers
Your Ranch or Mine? by Cindy Kirk
Mother in Training by Marie Ferrarella
A Baby for the Bachelor by Victoria Pade
The One She Left Behind by Kristi Gold
Her Son's Hero by Vicki Essex

SHIPMENT 7

Once and Again by Brenda Harlen
Her Sister's Fiancé by Teresa Hill
Family at Stake by Molly O'Keefe
Adding Up to Marriage by Karen Templeton
Bachelor Dad by Roxann Delaney
It's That Time of Year by Christine Wenger

SHIPMENT 8

The Rancher's Christmas Princess by Christine Rimmer
Their Baby Miracle by Lillian Darcy
Mad About Max by Penny McCusker
No Ordinary Joe by Michelle Celmer
The Soldier's Baby Bargain by Beth Kery
The Maverick's Christmas Baby by Victoria Pade

HOMETOWN HEARTS

The Cowboy's Secret Son

TRISH MILBURN

ISBN-13: 978-0-373-21474-7

The Cowboy's Secret Son

This edition published by arrangement with Harlequin Books S.A.

For questions and comments about the quality of this book, please contact us at CustomerService@Harlequin.com.

Printed in U.S.A.

Trish Milburn writes contemporary romance for the Harlequin Western Romance line. She's a two-time Golden Heart® Award winner, a fan of walks in the woods and road trips, and a big geek girl, including being a dedicated Whovian and Browncoat. And from her earliest memories, she's been a fan of Westerns, be they historical or contemporary. There's nothing quite like a cowboy hero.

Grace Cameron, the heroine of *The Cowboy's Secret Son*, has two close, special friends who have helped her through the hardest times of her life. I'm fortunate to have had the same. So here's to my two oldest friends—love ya, Allison and Kristy!

Chapter One

A rolling sea of bluebonnets in full bloom flowed out from where Grace Cameron sat at a roadside table. Her son, Evan, ran back and forth, pretending to ride an imaginary horse. But not even his boyish antics could lift her mood today.

Once, hills blanketed in bluebonnets had soothed her, allowing her to believe there was hope and beauty in the world beyond her daily existence. Now, the sight of them and the town in the distance caused fear and uncertainty to swirl inside her like a Texas twister.

Texas. She looked toward the horizon, soaking in a tiny sliver of Texas's vast and varied expanse. When her parents had dragged her away nearly seven years ago, she'd thought she'd never see it again. Later, she'd avoided the state for fear she'd lose more than she already had. And yet here she sat gazing out across the spring-painted Hill Country, on the verge of taking the final step in a decision that she'd second-guessed every moment since she'd made it.

She glanced at Evan, at his miniature cowboy boots and hat, the pint-size Wrangler jeans, and couldn't help but smile despite her inner turmoil. When she'd told him they were taking a vacation to Texas, that he was going to attend Cowboy Camp for Kids, he'd transformed into a bouncing ball of joy and excitement. While other little boys his age were into *Star Wars* and anime cartoons, he loved the reruns of old Westerns. His favorite cartoon character was Woody from *Toy Story*. He thought horses were God's greatest creation and believed everyone should have at least one.

You couldn't fight DNA.

"You ready to go, kiddo?"

Evan stopped midgallop. "Are we almost there?"

She nodded and pointed across the field of wildflowers. "See that town?"

"Yeah."

"That's Blue Falls. The camp is just a few miles on the other side."

His face lit up so much Grace wouldn't have been surprised if he started glowing. He raced to the car and was inside strapping on his seat belt by the time she managed to stand. She stared toward Blue Falls a bit longer, at the waterfalls that gave the town its name, the shimmer off the lake around which the town was built. Thousands of tourists flocked here each year, and all she wanted to do was turn around and leave it far behind.

But this trip wasn't about what she wanted. It was about what was best for her son.

Her feet felt as if they were encased in wet, heavy concrete as she headed for the car. She placed her hand on her stomach as if the action would calm the nausea plaguing her.

As she drove through Blue Falls, it felt familiar, and yet not. Some businesses she remembered from her youth were gone, others still there. She'd swear the same old coots were sitting out in front of the Primrose Café swapping probably the same old stories. The Blue Falls Music Hall had gotten a sorely needed facelift in the intervening years.

Taking in the view of her hometown was a little like having an out-of-body experience.

She wasn't the same Grace Cameron who'd lived here before, but that didn't keep a flood of old feelings from washing into every part of her body.

Evan stretched toward the window as far as his seat belt would let him. "I don't see any cowboys." The disappointment in his tone made Grace want to laugh and cry at the same time.

"Don't worry, they're around. A lot of these people are probably on vacation, like us." No doubt here for the popular wildflower tours. The appearance of the bluebonnets in March of each year made people crazy for wildflowers.

"Oh."

Grace looked at the faces they passed, too, searching for someone familiar.

Searching for Nathan.

For what seemed like the millionth time, she imagined all the ways he might respond when he found out he had a son. Shock. Disbelief. Anger. Probably all three. And he'd be entitled to each one.

She shook her head. No sense in torturing herself with possibilities. She'd find out the reality soon enough.

They waited at the last stoplight while a tour bus made the wide turn onto Main Street. The words *Wildflower Tours* stretched down the side of the bus, and little painted bluebonnets peeked out from around the letters. Grace wondered what it would be like to visit Blue Falls without any previous ties to the town or the people here.

"The light's green, Mom."

"Oops." She reined in her wandering thoughts and proceeded through the intersection.

They began the winding climb out of Blue Falls, and before she was ready—would she ever be ready?—they reached the Vista Hills Guest Ranch. Her palms grew sweaty against the steering wheel as she made the turn and started down the driveway lined with cedar and gnarled live oak trees.

Panic threatened to overwhelm her. What was she doing here?

She was here because Evan had a father.

And Nathan had a son.

Someday that relationship might be the most important one in the world—to her, at least.

When she rounded the last curve that brought her within view of the heart of the ranch, she had to take a deep breath. She didn't want Evan to sense how nervous she was. He might be only six, but he was observant and not easily fooled. As she pulled into a parking space next to the ranch office, Grace noticed a few other families with small children. They really were here for a vacation, to allow their kids a bit of cowboy fun. How she wished the days ahead would be that simple for her.

She eyed the other guests, but from her vantage point she couldn't tell if Laney and her daughter, Cheyenne, were among them. Grace didn't know if she could have come here without Laney for moral support.

"Mom, look! Horses!"

Grace looked toward the barns and surrounding corrals, remembering their locations as if she'd been here only yesterday. Half a dozen horses stood in the fenced enclosure next to the stables, and two families were gathered there as their little ones climbed up the fence for a better view. She noticed a man in jeans and a cowboy hat inside the fence talking to the group, but from this distance she couldn't tell if it was Nathan, one of his brothers, or an employee.

"Can we go look at the horses?"

"In a few minutes. We have to check in first."

"But, Mom!"

"Honey, the horses aren't going anywhere. You want to see our cabin, don't you?"

"Not as much as the horses."

The way he said it, all dramatic and pouty-faced, caused a laugh to escape her. Evan met her eyes in the rearview mirror, not at all amused.

Grace shook her head as she got out of the car. If she gave Evan a couple of minutes, he'd forget being put out with her and move on to admiring something else.

Evan's boots clonked on the wooden front steps of the office, and Grace wondered if Nathan had looked like that when he was young. A full-grown cowboy in his mind but only a little boy in truth.

With another deep breath, Grace opened the door and followed Evan inside.

"Well, hello there, young man," the older woman at the front desk said when she spotted Evan.

"Hello. I'm here to be a cowboy."

Merline Teague laughed, totally unaware she was talking to her grandson. Grace's throat went uncomfortably dry as she realized they'd just stepped beyond the point of no return.

"Well, then, you've come to the right place. What's your name, cowboy?"

"Evan Cameron."

"Nice to meet you, Evan Cameron."

Evan flicked up the front of his tan hat the way he'd seen movie-star cowboys do in all those old films. Merline paused as she reached for the appointment book, looking at him a moment longer as if she'd seen something that surprised her. Grace held her breath as her heart did its best to crack her ribs with its frantic beating.

Merline consulted her reservation book then looked at Grace for the first time. "Grace?"

"Yes, ma'am."

Merline glanced at Evan again, but only for a brief moment. "It's so good to see you. Been a long time."

"Yes, ma'am." Jeez, could she say nothing else?

Merline waved her hand in a "no need for that" type of gesture. "You're a grown woman now. Call me Merline."

"Yes…" Grace caught herself before she three-peated her response.

Merline eyed her reservation book again while Grace marveled at how little Nathan's mother had changed. She was still trim and fit with a tan that spoke of lots of time spent outdoors. She wasn't the type of woman to color her hair, but she didn't need to because she had gorgeous silver hair cut in a bob just below her ears. She was casual and classy at the same time, a woman comfortable in her skin and her surroundings.

"So you're living in Arkansas now," Merline said.

Grace could almost imagine the unspoken words. *Always wondered where you and your family disappeared to.*

"Moved there after college. My best friend was from the area, so we decided to set up shop there."

"What do you do?" Merline pulled a key from a rack behind her.

"Interior design."

"Oh, I bet that's fun. I love watching all those design shows on HGTV. I start watching one, and the next thing you know three hours have passed."

"Me, too."

"Even when you do it all day?"

Grace nodded. "Can't seem to get enough of it, I guess." She supposed she was still trying to fill her life with beautiful things after so many years of being forbidden them.

Merline handed Grace the key and a sheet of paper. "You're in cabin twelve. Just take the drive behind the office."

"I remember."

Merline smiled, looking as if dozens of questions were swirling unspoken inside her. Could she possibly have put things together that quickly, especially since Grace and Nathan had never really dated? Grace fought the urge to grab the key and run, telling herself that her anxiety was causing her to see things that weren't there. She tried not to think how Evan might have inherited his keen sense of observation from his paternal grandmother.

"That's the schedule for the weekend," Merline said as she pointed to the paper she'd handed Grace. "You're just in time to get settled before the tour."

"Will we get to see the horses?" Evan was bouncing on the balls of his feet, unable to keep still.

Merline smiled at him. "Yes, sir. Lots of horses."

"Awesome!"

Grace laughed right along with Merline.

"Excited, isn't he?"

Grace pushed down the front of Evan's hat. "Yes, he's talked about nothing else since I told him he was going to Cowboy Camp."

"Our boys were crazy for horses at that age, too. Still are."

The mention of the Teague brothers ratcheted Grace's anxiety up another notch. She placed her hand on Evan's back. "Let's go, pardner. We need to unpack."

This time, Evan didn't express how unpacking was way down his list of things he wanted to do. Instead, he turned and headed for the door.

"Good to see you again, Grace."

Was there an extra layer of meaning in those words, or was she imagining it?

Grace met the other woman's gaze only briefly. "You, too, ma— Merline." She stepped toward the door before she could stumble over something besides Merline's name.

Just as she and Evan reached the door, it swung open and a much larger version of her son stepped inside.

"Mom, it's a cowboy," Evan said in awe.

Yes, it was indeed a cowboy. And Nathan Teague still took her breath away.

Nathan looked down at the little guy tricked out in full cowboy attire. Whose idea had it been to let the ranch be overrun by munchkins all week? Oh, yeah, his. Temporary insanity, had to be. Already, two campers had cried when the horses got too close. One had screamed so loudly his parents had apologized profusely and headed back to Austin so they could check in to a hotel with a nice, big pool. He looked at their latest arrival and wondered how this one would react. Oh, well, he had to make the best of the situation.

He touched the front of his hat. "Looks to me like there are two cowboys in here."

The little boy scanned the office before he realized what Nathan meant. He smiled so wide, Nathan couldn't help but smile back. Maybe there was hope yet.

"Nathan, you remember Grace Cameron?"

He looked at his mom, who nodded at a woman standing to the side of the little boy. It took a few clicks of the cogs in his brain for the truth to slip into place. But beyond the stylish, beautiful blonde in front of him, he could just make out the girl who'd been his algebra tutor. A girl he'd made love to and then pretended like it didn't happen.

A girl who had disappeared without a trace, without a word. And now she reappeared just as suddenly and without warning.

"Grace." For some reason, his brain couldn't force more than her name out of his mouth.

"Nathan, good to see you."

She only met his eyes for the barest hint of a moment before she turned her attention to the boy.

"Yours?" he asked.

"Yes." Her voice sounded small, the same

as he remembered it. So a part of that teenage girl remained below the surface of the woman she'd grown into.

The little boy looked up at Grace. "Mom, do you know the cowboy?"

"Yes, honey," she said, her voice stronger. "This is Nathan Teague. We used to go to school together."

The kid looked as if his mother had just told him she knew his favorite football player or superhero.

Grace placed her hands on the boy's shoulders in what looked like a protective gesture. Maybe she was nervous that he might get hurt here, a common worry among the parents he'd met so far today. He resisted the odd urge to reassure her.

"Nathan, this little cowboy is Evan," she said.

Nathan extended his hand, and Evan shook it without hesitation.

"You've got a good grip there."

If possible, Evan grinned even wider.

"Were you good at school, too?" Evan asked.

Nathan laughed. "Not as good as your mom. In fact, she had to help me pass one of my classes."

Evan nodded. "She helps me with my homework, too."

"You're mighty young to have homework."

"You'd be surprised," Grace said. "School has changed a lot in just a few years." So had Grace. Or had her voice always been that pretty, the audible equivalent of a gorgeous spring day, and he'd never noticed it cloaked in her shyness? He had the oddest sensation that he'd like to hear her read to him. This time when she met his eyes, they held for a little longer, allowing him to appreciate their pale blue color. When she seemed to realize this, she ushered her son toward the door. Having forgotten what had brought him inside, he followed in her wake.

"Are you back in Blue Falls?" he asked.

"Just a little vacation."

Evan spotted the horses and a few more kids down by the corrals. "Mom, can I go see the horses? Please!"

She looked about to refuse, with an edge of concern pulling at her features. It wasn't the first time he'd seen that look today. "He'll be safe. Simon and Dad are down there."

Grace still looked unsure but finally relented. "Okay." Evan shot off like an Olympic sprinter. "But be careful," she called after him.

"He seems excited to be here."

"You have no idea. I swear he's John Wayne reincarnated."

He chuckled. "There are worse things."

"Yeah."

He followed as she walked slowly toward a bench overlooking the stables and corrals. She sank onto it as though she was utterly exhausted.

"You okay? You look tired."

"Just a long drive today."

Instinct told him it was more than that, but if she didn't want to share, it wasn't any of his business. Suddenly, he wanted to apologize for the idiot he'd been back in high school, but she'd probably think him an even bigger idiot for bringing it up now when she'd obviously moved on.

He didn't sit beside her. Rather, he leaned against a nearby oak tree. They both watched as Evan climbed up on the fence rails and reached over to pet a big blonde mare named Dolly.

"At least he's not running away in terror like some of the kids," he said.

"Unfortunately, he has no fear. I took him to a rodeo once, and I firmly believe he would have climbed onto the back of one of the bucking horses and given it a whirl."

Nathan laughed. "Fearlessness can come in handy."

"I don't want him to be scared of everything, but a little healthy, self-preserving fear would be nice."

Nathan looked over at Grace's golden blond hair. When he'd known her before, it'd been long and straight down her back. Now, she had it cut in a shorter, wavy style that suited her. "Well, it doesn't look like he's caused you to go gray yet."

Grace lifted her hand to her hair, and he noticed she wasn't wearing a wedding ring. "No, not yet."

A little girl in pink cowgirl boots, a pink shirt with fringe and a pink cowgirl hat climbed up on the fence next to Evan and started petting Dolly, too. She struck up a conversation with Evan, unintelligible at this distance.

"Hey, we've got two kids who actually like the horses. This week might work out yet."

"Do you usually have lots of kids afraid of the horses?"

Nathan shrugged. "Don't know. This is the first time we've done the camp. Maybe the last."

Grace didn't respond. Despite looking tired, she didn't seem terribly relaxed. In fact, her back was as straight as if she was tied to a fence post. She clasped her hands together in her lap so tightly that her knuckles had gone white.

"You sure you're okay? Can I get you something to drink?"

"He's yours."

Her quick response made no sense. "What?"

Grace turned her head slowly, met his gaze. "Evan. He's your son."

Chapter Two

All the breathable oxygen disappeared from around Nathan. At least it felt that way.

"What?" He stared at Grace, thinking he couldn't possibly have heard her correctly.

Grace clasped her hands into a tight ball in her lap and took a deep breath. "Evan is your son."

"That's not possible."

She looked up at him. "I assure you it is."

Nathan snatched his hat off and ran his fingers through his hair. He took a couple of steps away from Grace, away from the words she'd spoken. The boy she claimed was his son was now feeding the horse a carrot with Simon's help. A wild storm of denial and curiosity whirled within him.

"You got pregnant that night at the party?" he asked without turning back toward Grace.

"Yes."

Heat rushed through him. "And instead of telling me then, you decided to run away?"

"I didn't have a choice."

She said it so matter-of-factly that an unusual anger roared inside him. He spun back toward her, met her gaze. "You always have a choice."

"Maybe you did, when you decided to pretend nothing had happened between us."

Despite his anger, he winced at the sharpness of that truth.

Grace shifted her gaze toward the stand of trees opposite where she sat. "But I didn't when my parents literally dragged me away in the middle of the night in shame."

He'd met her parents once, and could all too easily imagine them doing such a thing. But he didn't want to feel sorry for her. Six years had passed since then, years in which she'd cheated him by keeping the existence of a son from him. If Evan was his. Maybe she was mistaken.

"How do you know he's mine?"

She laughed, but it wasn't the type of laugh born of amusement. "You're really asking me that question?"

He crossed his arms and stared at her, every muscle in his body tense. "Yes. You show up here unannounced and tell me some boy I've never seen is my son, and I'm supposed to just believe that?"

Grace shifted on the bench so that she more fully faced him. "Think about it. Do you remember me having guys lining up to sleep with me back in high school?"

"I don't know what you did. You could have met someone after you left here."

She shook her head, and something about her expression made him feel as if she thought him the most clueless man in the world. "I pretty much lived under lock and key when I lived here, and it only got worse after we left, after my parents discovered I was pregnant. I had to sneak out a window to come to that party."

"Why did you?"

She didn't immediately answer. Instead, she seemed to think about it as she let her gaze fall away from him. "Because I liked you. And I thought maybe you liked me."

He didn't know what to say to that. The silence stretched to an uncomfortable length. He plopped the hat back on his head and shoved his hands in his jean's pockets. "I don't know how to react or what to say. I feel like I just got hit with a cattle prod and a stampede all at once."

"You don't have to do anything, at least not now."

He glanced at her, trying to read this woman he didn't even know anymore. Had he ever? She was no more the girl who'd helped him raise his algebra grade so he could play football than one of the fence posts around the corral. That girl had barely been able to meet his eyes, even on that night he'd made love to her.

This woman marched onto his ranch and pronounced him the father of her little cowboy wannabe.

Man, he felt as if his head was going to explode.

"What does that mean, not now?"

"I'm not looking for money, or even your help in raising him. I'm doing fine on my own."

"Then, why tell me at all?"

"Because I'm all he has, and if something ever happens to me, I want him to have somewhere to go."

The way she sounded as though he was nothing more than a back-up plan caused his anger to swell. "And you thought of the sperm donor?"

She gasped, and her eyes went wide. "Nathan, that's not how I think of you."

"It's not?"

"No."

"Could have fooled me. What if nothing happens to you, Grace? I get nothing? I'm just supposed to forget you dropped this little bombshell on my head?"

"Of course not." She appeared flustered, as if she hadn't anticipated him putting up a fuss. "I just wanted you to know."

He looked toward the corral when he heard youthful giggles. Evan and the little pink girl were laughing, at what he couldn't tell. "Why now? I'm assuming you didn't just leave your parents' house."

"I… I just finally got up the nerve. I realized it wasn't responsible to be a single parent and not make plans in case something happened to me."

He shook his head and shifted his eyes back to her. "You could have called. Hell, written a letter or something."

"I thought about it, picked up the phone I don't know how many times."

"And you decided just dropping by was better?"

"I didn't know. I honestly didn't know if I could go through with it. I almost turned around half a dozen times."

"Good to know I could still be in the bloody dark about having a kid."

This time, she winced. "Telling you wasn't as easy as you obviously think it should have been."

He shifted from one foot to the other, cursing himself for the fool he'd been that long-ago night. One more idiot kid who couldn't keep his pants zipped. "Did I really treat you so badly that you'd keep my son from me?"

"This isn't about you, Nathan."

"Obviously." He had to get away, find some air to refill his lungs. Calm the hell down. He couldn't think when he was so close to this woman spouting words that could change his life so dramatically. When he could see the boy who might very well be the beginning of a new generation of Teagues. "I've got work to do."

He stalked down the hill but didn't head for the barn. Instead, he made for his truck. Nothing like a drive up to the more remote area of the ranch to help him untangle his thoughts.

If only he'd taken time to think seven years ago.

That had not gone well. Grace sat on the bench, bone weary and wishing she could turn back the clock even an hour. One would think, after all the time she'd spent contemplating various ways she could tell Nathan about Evan, she'd end up doing something other than just blurting it out at the first opportunity.

She didn't let her doubts get the better of her, tempting her into believing she'd made a mistake in telling Nathan about his son. It was the right thing to do, for many reasons, but she wished he'd stuck around longer so she could explain further. Part of her couldn't blame him for his reaction. If she were in his spot, she had no idea how she'd react.

There was no going back now, though. She'd simply have to figure out how to progress from her clumsy start.

"Didn't go how you'd hoped, huh?"

Grace looked up to see Laney Stuart had approached without her noticing. "I don't know why I bothered running scenarios in my head because my brain and mouth staged a coup and abandoned them all."

Laney sat on the bench next to Grace. "Well, at least it's done."

"It's far from done. I fear it's just the beginning."

"Then at least you can stop imagining how he'll react. Now you know."

"And I feel loads better," Grace said, her voice full of sarcasm. "I thought you were here for moral support, not stating the obvious."

Laney squeezed Grace's hand. "I am, sweetie. I'll listen anytime you need to talk."

Grace squeezed back. "It's good to see you. It's been too long."

"You just miss my French toast."

Grace managed a small laugh. "If my stomach ever calms down, I fully expect you to make me some."

Laney leaned back with a dramatic sigh. "You only love me for my culinary skills."

"If I remember correctly, French toast is the extent of your culinary skills."

Laney playfully punched Grace in the arm. "That's not true."

"Oh, you're right. I forgot mac and cheese—from a box."

Laney gave Grace a narrow-eyed stare. "Tell

me again why I like you, why I took a week off from work to come to the-middle-of-nowhere Texas."

"I babysat your daughter so you could study?"

"Hmm, seems I remember doing something similar for you."

She had indeed. Laney had been a single mom grad student trying to finish her degree and plan for a wedding to her long-distance boyfriend when she'd advertised for two roommates. Grace, along with Emily Stringer, one of Grace's fellow interior design students and her current business partner, had answered the ad.

Grace still swore something cosmic had brought the three of them together. She'd bonded with Emily over their shared love of interior design, and with Laney over their single motherhood. Laney and Emily had similar personalities: strong, determined and quick with snappy comebacks. Considering the roommate horror stories she'd heard during her years of college, she'd won the roomie lottery.

While Evan and Cheyenne had played, Grace and her two best friends had studied, laughed, planned for their futures and shared their deepest secrets. Laney and Emily were the loving, nurturing, fun sisters her own had never been.

"It's so good to see you," Grace said, growing serious. "You have no idea how much it means to me to have you here."

"I think I do. You were there for me on some of my most frightening days. And you know Emily would be here, too, if you hadn't threatened her with bodily harm if she closed the doors."

"I know, but our business is too new for both of us to be AWOL on the customers we do have. Plus, she's already been there for me so many times."

"Don't worry about that now. Focus on what you came here to do."

Grace sighed. "I doubt I could think about anything else for more than two seconds if I tried."

"You'll get through this, just like everything else."

"I hope you're right." Grace took a deep breath then stood. "I better get us settled in our cabin."

"He'll come around. May take some time and he might be angry for a while, but he'll get over it. And if not, I'll be forced to kick his ass."

Grace lifted an eyebrow. Of the three of them, Laney was by far the most girly.

"Okay, hire someone to kick his ass," Laney admitted.

Grace leaned down and gave Laney a quick hug before walking down the slight incline toward the stables. "Evan." When he turned at the sound of his name, she motioned for him to come to her. "Come on. We have to take our stuff to the cabin."

"But, Mom..."

"We'll be coming back in a bit. Now don't argue." Her last words came out a little sharper than she intended, so when he reached her she gave him a big smile and placed her arm lovingly around his shoulders. "I see you and Cheyenne found each other."

He grunted in confirmation but kept staring back at the corral. "Isn't she pretty? She ate sugar cubes right out of my hand!"

"Cheyenne?"

He looked at Grace as if she'd suddenly taken leave of her senses. "No! Eww. I was talking about Dolly, the horse."

"Oh, of course." Grace bit her lip to keep from laughing.

But as they got into the car and headed up the hill to the cabins, her urge to laugh faded away. When she thought about it, Evan really wasn't that different from his father. Back when she'd known the younger version of Nathan, he'd been more wrapped up in horses and football than he had in any girl, least of all her.

As Grace pulled up in front of their cabin, she realized she'd never been inside one of them. She'd come to the ranch several times while tutoring Nathan, but they'd been confined to the dining room in the main house where Merline could watch them. That had been one of her parents' conditions of her employment—that she and Nathan never be left alone. As if the two of them would suddenly go off and do all manner of sinful, indecent things. Little did they know their tight leash contributed to her doing the thing they most feared.

"Mom? Are you getting out?"

Grace shook off the dust of the past and realized Evan had already unbuckled himself and gotten out of the car. He stared at her through the open passenger window.

"Yeah, sweetie." She needed to pull herself together, regroup. She'd stumbled through her initial meeting with Nathan and the big reveal, but there was no going back for a do-over.

With Evan's help, she got their bags inside. When she dropped their biggest suitcase on the bed, she noticed Evan had climbed into a chair to look at some framed photos on the wall. She walked up behind him and immediately spotted Nathan in one of the photos, sitting astride a horse in early-morning light. His face wasn't fully visible, probably wouldn't even be recognizable to the casual observer, but she knew it instantly. Despite that one night together, they'd never been a couple. But that didn't mean she hadn't memorized every contour of his face. It'd been all she could do to not stare at him in class and when they sat across from each other during the tutoring sessions.

But that was a long time ago. A lifetime. Evan's lifetime.

"Come on, cowboy. Let's get unpacked so we can get back for the tour." Yes, this trip was about ensuring Evan's future, but for him it was supposed to be a dream vacation. And she planned to let him have exactly that. She wouldn't allow her own issues to ruin her son's big adventure.

"When will I be able to ride a horse?" Evan asked as he placed his clothes in one of the lower drawers.

"Probably not today."

"Aww, man. Why not?"

"There are lots of things the cowboys have to

show you first." Like how to stay safe around those horses.

Grace shoved her instinctual worry about Evan's safety down. There was a delicate balance between protecting him and smothering him the way Bob and Ruth Cameron had her and her siblings. And she refused to follow in their footsteps.

"You just have to take it one thing at a time, squirt," she said. "I guarantee, you'll like all of it."

As they finally finished unpacking, Evan was on the verge of hopping with excitement and anticipation to get back to the main part of the ranch. Grace wondered if she'd ever possessed that sort of giddy energy. It was infectious though, and by the time they returned to the area with the barn and corrals, she was looking forward to the afternoon, too.

That anticipation faltered a bit when she spotted Nathan striding out of the barn straight toward them. Her heart thumped wildly in her chest. Surely he wouldn't reveal his paternity to Evan right here in front of everyone. She started to step forward, to force him inside the barn so they could talk, but he stopped abruptly.

"Good afternoon, folks," he said to the entire gathering. "Welcome to our first ever Cowboy

Camp for Kids. If you've had a chance to look at your schedules, you'll see we've got a lot lined up for you this week. Unless anyone has any questions, we're going to start with a little tour." Nathan turned without even making eye contact with Grace or glancing at Evan. "If you'll follow me."

Grace couldn't help the bite of concern. Would Nathan reject Evan? She didn't think she could bear that.

"Don't borrow trouble," Laney said low beside her. "Just go with the flow for now, see what happens."

With a deep breath, Grace followed along with all the other kids and parents, hoping to make it through the afternoon's activities. Maybe she'd find a chance to talk to Nathan more, force him to agree to her request for silence on the subject of Evan's paternity. She refused to think about how he might react to that request. Not well if his actions so far were any indication. But she could only handle one big change at a time, and just seeing Nathan and Evan so close to each other was making her pulse jittery. Every time Nathan opened his mouth to talk about stalls or daily chores on a ranch or veterinary care for the horses, she had the unreasonable fear that he was going to reveal all to Evan.

Laney pointed her smooth, manicured hand toward where Evan and Cheyenne hung on Nathan's every word. "Kindred spirits."

"Yeah. Even though I don't think Evan would admit it now."

"At the 'eww, girls' stage?"

"So he says, and I'd like to keep him there for at least two decades."

Laney shook her head, causing her pretty brunette bob to sway. "Hard to believe they once shared a playpen."

They paused and listened as Cheyenne asked if Nathan had ever ridden in the rodeo. Grace could have answered this for him, that he'd done a few local things for fun but never seriously. At least that was the answer when she'd still lived here.

Laney shook her head. "I wondered how long it would be before she got to a rodeo question."

"Still likes rodeo?" Grace asked as they moved out of the barn and into one of the corrals where Dolly and another horse stood saddled.

"So much so you'd swear she was raised on a ranch instead of in downtown Chicago."

Grace nodded toward Evan. "I blame reruns of Westerns on the Hallmark Channel."

Laney laughed. "And I blame all those rodeos they run on country music channels." Just then Cheyenne looked back at them, smiled wide and waved. They returned both the smile and the wave. "But I can't really complain. They got us through some tough times."

Grace knew Laney was referring to how Chey had been a sick little girl for about a year. She'd had a heart condition that, thankfully, doctors had been able to fix once she got old enough. But the months of waiting for her to get to an age where the procedure would be safer to perform had been agonizing.

The memory made Grace's own heart squeeze. She couldn't fathom having something threaten Evan's life. "She's still doing okay?"

"Oh, yes. Totally healthy." Laney found a spot on a bench next to the fence and sat down.

Still tired, Grace joined her as Nathan continued telling the kids about the parts of a saddle.

"It still seems so weird to me that watching rodeos was the only thing that would keep her calm when she was sick. Not cartoons, not soothing music. Rodeo. Of all the things. But there she was, glued to the TV anytime it was on. I still have some of the ones I recorded back then." Laney shook her head. "I don't know where she gets it. Certainly not from her father or me."

"No hidden rodeoing in your past, huh?"

Laney laughed. "Not even a stint as rodeo queen."

Grace made the mistake of looking at Nathan at the moment he pushed up the front brim of his hat. The motion was so like Evan's it took her breath away.

"Grace?"

"Huh?"

"You okay?"

"Uh, yeah. Just tired."

Worry descended on Laney's features. "Are you sure?"

"Yeah, I'm fine." For now. She shifted her gaze away from her friend's concern, not wanting to think about why it was there. Once you'd battled the cancer monster, it was hard to get past the idea that it might jump out at you again.

Nathan stepped aside as Merline walked to the front of the group. "I hope everyone is hungry because we're putting on a big Texas-style barbecue for you all tonight. We'll get started in about an hour, so that gives you time to go and freshen up. Just come on up behind the house, and you'll get to mix and mingle, meet the rest of the family and the hands."

Grace's nerves fired. The rest of the Teagues. As in Evan's grandparents and uncles. "Excuse me."

"Sure," Laney said. "See you at dinner?"

Grace nodded, but her attention was tracking Nathan as he headed back through the barn. She hurried after him, but his long legs had carried him almost halfway through before she caught him.

"Nathan, I need to talk to you."

"Not now, Grace," he said, his voice clipped and without any hint of warmth. He didn't slow or look at her.

She grabbed his wrist and stopped, forcing him to do the same. When his eyes met hers, she didn't waver. "Yes, now."

Chapter Three

Grace held her breath until Nathan finally let out a slow sigh and nodded. He motioned for her to follow him. After a quick glance back to see that Evan was busy talking to some of the other kids, she accompanied Nathan as they walked out of the front of the barn and down the driveway a short distance. When they were out of earshot of the other guests, he propped one booted foot and his forearms up on the fence and gazed out into the distance. The rigidity of his stance told her he was struggling to contain his anger.

"I believe you," he said.

"What?"

"I believe he's mine. You never seemed like the type of person to lie. Not outright anyway."

The half compliment was unexpected, but she didn't assign too much weight to it. He probably didn't even mean it as a compliment if his tone was any indication, rather just a truth. Better she think of it that way. Nathan Teague was from another part of her life, and was in her present life only for a brief time out of necessity, nothing more.

"It's been seven years. I could have changed."

He glanced at her, all of her, and it made her skin flush. She hoped he couldn't see it, or attributed it to her being fair and out in the Texas sun.

"Yes, you've changed on the surface, but I don't believe people change at their core. Even if they do make bad decisions."

Grace did her best to ignore how his words stung. No matter how he felt, she'd never think of Evan as a mistake. She moved closer to the wooden fence and propped her arms on the top slat, as well. "You barely knew me."

"True. But I tend to pay attention to my gut instincts."

"What's it telling you about me now?" Out of the corner of her eye she saw him watching her, but she didn't face him.

"That something changed in your life, some reason you finally decided to tell me I have a son."

Grace winced at the harsh edge to his words, but she also acknowledged he was entitled to it. No matter what had transpired between the two of them in the past, it was a big thing to have a child and not know about it. She pushed away those old feelings of hurt and abandonment that had deluged her after that night with Nathan, when he'd avoided her eyes in the school hallways as if he didn't know her. She was a different person now, an adult, so maybe he was, too.

"I guess I grew up, realized that I have responsibilities. And one of those is ensuring my son's future in case something happens to me." She sensed his next question, so she continued before he could speak. "You know, I could die in a car wreck tomorrow."

He was quiet for a moment, and she wondered if he could tell she was hiding something. She just wasn't ready to reveal everything, afraid she'd start crying if she thought too much about the cancer returning. She wanted Nathan to agree to care for Evan should the need arise because he felt a kinship to his son, not because of pity for her. She never wanted Evan to feel like a charity case.

"What about your family?"

"I haven't talked to them since I turned eighteen."

"You've been alone this whole time?"

"I've had Evan, and friends once I went to college. My friend Emily and I started a business together, interior design. So I have a good life." Evan and the fact that she'd made her life what she wanted it to be were what had gotten her through bad doctor reports and body-draining chemo. Only in her darkest moments, when she'd succumbed to the fear that the disease might win, had she yearned for more. For a man to love and be loved by. Someone to offer her support, hold her hand during those endless hours lying in a hospital bed or curled into her own after a chemo session.

Nathan sighed and shook his head as if he couldn't believe any of this was happening. "Why didn't you tell me sooner? I had a right to know."

She'd anticipated this question, considered so many different ways to answer it. Finally, she'd settled on the truth.

"I was scared."

"Of me?"

"No, and yes."

Nathan slipped his foot off the fence and turned toward her. "I wasn't that bad, Grace."

She wanted to say, "Yes, you really hurt me," but that wasn't what was important anymore. She didn't shift to face him, not sure if she could get through the next few minutes if she had to look him in the eye and see anger and accusations there.

"I was hurt, yes, but that's not why I made the choices I did." She picked at a splinter on the fence, gathering her courage to delve into a part of her life steeped in a lot of pain. "I had lost Evan once, and I couldn't bear the thought of it happening again."

"Lost him?"

"When I told my parents I was pregnant, well, I've never seen them so mad. They were ashamed I was their daughter, and I know if I'd been of legal age, they would have kicked me out then. Instead, they packed us up in the middle of the night and left town."

"You knew before you left Blue Falls? And you didn't tell me then? God, Grace. What were you thinking?"

"That the father of my child didn't want me, so he wouldn't want a baby, either." This time she didn't bother keeping the bite out of her words.

Nathan didn't respond, instead shifting his attention out across the pasture again. She didn't say anything either, and the silence stretched for tense seconds.

"Everyone wondered where you went," he finally said.

"I doubt everyone did." She couldn't help the bitter edge to her words, bits of the old hurt slipping out.

"I did."

Those simple words were so unexpected that she looked at him before thinking. And for a moment, she was that young girl again looking into the striking green eyes of the boy she loved with all her heart. The one she'd thought might love her back when he'd taken her in his arms and kissed her.

It took more effort than it should, but she pulled her gaze away and refocused on the glint off a pond in the distance.

"We went to Maryland, where my grandparents lived, lots of other people who were as devout as my parents." She hadn't planned to tell him everything, especially not at first, but she found herself spilling the details of those days. "I… I basically became a prisoner in my own home. I was forced to finish school homebound. My mother had nothing to do with it though.

My sister Sarah had to bring my lessons home from school, and I was on my own. I wasn't allowed to go anywhere. My parents did not talk to me, but they constantly used me as an example to my younger brothers and sisters of what happens when one 'descends into a life of sin.'"

Nathan made a sound of disgust, but Grace didn't acknowledge it. She had to get through this story so she could file it away forever and never have to tell it again.

"I think after a while, I began to believe everything they said. I was sick, miserable… lonely." And heartbroken.

"Why didn't you call me?"

"You'd made it clear you didn't want to talk to me."

"But Grace, a baby would have made a difference."

She turned toward him. "Would it? Would you have 'done the right thing' and married me?"

"Yes."

A sadness crept over Grace's heart. "How would it have helped me to go from one home where I wasn't wanted, just a duty to fulfill, to another?"

"Damn it, it wouldn't have been like that."

"Did you love me?"

He opened his mouth, but no words came out.

"I didn't think so. Plus, my parents had done a pretty good brainwashing job on me. You were nothing more than a rutting bull in their eyes."

"And you believed them?"

"You hadn't given me any reason not to. And when you're cut off from the world, you begin to believe whatever you're told."

"God, Grace." He paced a couple of steps away, ran his hand over his face.

She tried not to remember what that hand had felt like on her body, how her entire being had lit up like a million stars. She forced herself to remember how all those stars had gone black and cold the day after when he'd walked right by her as though she was a complete stranger. No expression, no eye contact, no recognition. She remembered stopping in the middle of the hallway, wondering if she'd simply dreamed it all. But a positive result on a home pregnancy test a few weeks later had convinced her their night together had been all too real.

"When it came time to have Evan, I had to deliver him at home just like my mother always had." All twelve times. "It was a hard birth. I probably should have been in a hospital. By the time it was over, I was only about half conscious. My mother said it was best to give him up for adoption. I had no strength to fight her, and she made it sound like he would have a good home, a family who loved him. At the time, it sounded like the right thing to do. I didn't want him growing up with my family."

"You gave him away?"

Grace hated the horrified disbelief in his voice, how it echoed the feelings she'd had herself after she'd recovered from the birth.

"My parents had damaged enough of us. I thought it would give him a chance. But..." Grace's voice broke, and it took her a few moments to bring her emotions back under control. "I thought I'd have the opportunity to say goodbye, but by the time I woke up he was gone. I never even got to hold him."

"What? How is that possible?"

Grace squeezed her hands into fists at the memory, the betrayal. "There's a law where newborns can be dropped off at hospitals or police stations, no questions asked. You just sign away the rights to the child, and my mother misrepresented him as hers. She just handed him over, turned her back and walked away from her first grandchild."

She ventured a glance at Nathan, and he looked stunned to the point of numbness—

a feeling with which she was intimately acquainted.

"I was so messed up, Nathan. They'd twisted my mind, and I had bad postpartum. There were points when I just wanted to die. And then on my eighteenth birthday, my parents told me to leave, that I was no longer their responsibility. I was basically dead to them. They forced me out the front door with literally nothing other than the clothes I was wearing. They kept the rest to give to my sisters."

She hazarded a glance at Nathan. He looked like he wanted to punch something. "What did you do?"

"The first thing I did was walk to the nearest police station and told them my mother had stolen my baby. It was like the moment I was free of that house, all the brain fuzziness went away. I can't explain it. While the police checked out my story, I engaged in what I like to call creative living." She smiled a little at that, felt a well of pride at the memory of how she'd taken over her life. "I slept and ate at shelters, got a job at a restaurant, added some more clothes from a church clothing bank. And I applied for college. Being as poor as a person can be, I got a full ride."

"So you had food and a place to live."

She gripped the top of the fence. "And I got Evan back."

Nathan exhaled as if he'd been holding his breath, afraid of where her story was heading. "He hadn't been adopted? I thought newborns went quickly."

"There's a lot of paperwork in that. It takes time. A child has to thrive in a potential adoptive home for at least six months before they'll allow an adoption to go through. It was so close, Nathan." She fought tears at the memory. "The first six months were almost up when the potential mom was diagnosed with MS. I mean, I'm so sorry it happened to her, it's horrible, but they canceled the adoption, and the six months had to start over. I got him back two months into that. I'd missed the first eight months of his life, but I had him back. I was able to finally hold my son."

"Our son."

She met Nathan's eyes, wondering how he was processing all this information, this crazy story that was her life after him. "Yes, our son."

Those two words—*our son*—had a ring of intimacy, but it wasn't one they shared anymore. Never really had.

Nathan was silent for several moments, ones

in which Grace could hear the kids laughing and talking on the other side of the barn. She experienced a moment of panic when she wondered if Nathan had told any of the members of his family about Evan. Would they say something to Evan? She glanced through the barn, but he wasn't visible.

"Why didn't you tell me then?" Nathan asked, drawing her attention back to them and their conversation. His anger at being shut out was still evident in his tone, might always be there. Especially when he heard everything she had to say.

"I was young and afraid to let anyone in, afraid someone else would try to take Evan away from me."

"By someone, you mean me."

"And your family."

"You must not think much of us."

"It wasn't that. I always liked your family, was really envious of you. But you have to understand. I'd just been through the equivalent of psychological torture, at least from my point of view. The way I was looking at things then, I thought that if you knew about Evan, you'd be able to take him from me because you had money, family support, all the things I didn't have. I'm not saying it was right, but it's how my brain was working then."

"We wouldn't have stolen him from you. We're not like that. Family is the most important thing to us."

"Yes, but I'm not family."

The sound of the kids' voices grew louder, coming closer. Nathan shifted, made to leave. She touched his arm, praying he wouldn't think her cold and heartless for what she was about to ask of him but prepared to deal with it if he did.

"Nathan, I need you to not tell Evan you're his father."

His expression tightened. "What?"

"I didn't come here to make any big changes. We have a good life in Little Rock, one we're going back to soon."

Nathan shook his head. "I don't believe you. You come here, tell me I have a son, but that I can't let him know that."

Grace let her hand fall away after she realized she was still touching Nathan. "He's too young to understand, and I don't want him getting attached and then hurt when we leave."

Nathan threw up his hands in frustration. "Then why tell me at all?"

"I told you why."

"Oh, yeah, so you'll have someone on the line to take care of him in case an asteroid falls on your head. Great to know you think so highly of me. I'm okay only if you're dead and there's no other choice."

Grace flinched. She understood his anger, really she did, but she couldn't bear the thought of Evan attaching himself to Nathan and having his little heart broken when she took him away from his father.

"It's not like that."

"Isn't it?"

"No, Nathan. I just…please, I want him to have a good time here. He's been looking forward to this so much."

"And you think if you tell him I'm his daddy that it'll ruin his camping experience?" Such bitterness laced his every word.

"No. I don't know. Can we please just give it a few days, let him get settled?" And maybe by then Nathan would have calmed down enough to see her side of things, that stability was the best thing for Evan as he grew up.

Wouldn't having a father be the best thing?

She told the voice in her head to shut up, that she knew what she was doing.

Nathan stared at the kids emerging from the barn, Evan among them.

"Nathan?" Grace held her breath as Evan got closer, as he broke away from the others and ran toward her and Nathan.

"Mom, guess what!"

Grace hesitated in responding. She couldn't tear her gaze away from Nathan, silently pleading with him to keep their secret, at least for now.

"I'll see you two at dinner," Nathan said, then stalked away.

Grace let out a sigh of relief. She didn't know how long he'd keep quiet, but for now she could breathe again. At least as much as she was able to watching the best-looking man she'd ever seen walk away from her. If she'd known the grown-up Nathan could make her heart somersault the way the teenage Nathan had, she wasn't sure if she would have had the willpower to come back to Blue Falls.

She felt the first chink in the armor around her heart fall away.

Nathan tried not to stare. Not at Grace, with whom he was equal parts angry and, damn it, fascinated. She was so different from the girl he'd known.

And not at Evan, his son. Every time he thought about it, his knees grew weak.

He kept glancing over to where they sat at one of the picnic tables, talking to another of the mothers and the little girl in the pink cowgirl getup. When he noticed Grace laughing at something, he couldn't look away. How could she laugh after what she'd kept from him? After all she'd been through?

That same rush of hot anger he'd felt when she'd told him about how her mother had given away Evan surged through him again. He might be furious at Grace for stealing the first years of his son's life from him, but at least she hadn't tossed Evan away like garbage. His hands clenched into fists. He'd known her parents were strict, odd even, but he'd never imagined they were capable of such cruelty.

Part of him understood why Grace had made the decisions she had, but part of him couldn't get past that she hadn't even tried to tell him about Evan. She'd lost eight months with Evan, but he'd been cheated out of six years with his son. He didn't know if he could forgive her for that.

He noticed his mother making her way through the crowd, stopping to chat with their guests for the week as well as Trudy, the ranch's longtime cook. Grudgingly willing to keep Grace's secret for the time being, until he could figure out how to change her mind and make sure she didn't flee with Evan, he shifted his attention away from her and began filling a plate for himself. Not that he was going to be able to even taste the barbecue, baked beans or potato salad. He doubted even the apple pie would make an impression today.

He knew he should mingle, go and sit with the guests, but he just couldn't handle that right now. Truth be told, he wished he could send them all home and concentrate on more important matters, like convincing Grace that Evan deserved to know his father. That she couldn't parade his son in front of his nose and expect him not to say anything. He just had to convince her that he wasn't going to take Evan away from her.

His mom, now with a full plate of her own, sat beside him. He forced himself to concentrate on his food.

"Pretty nice group of folks," his mom said as she scooped up a forkful of potato salad.

"Yeah, seem to be."

"Was a surprise to see Grace."

Man, don't go down this road. "Yeah. Said her boy likes cowboys a lot." He forced himself not to look their direction.

They were silent for a few moments while

they both ate, but he gradually became aware of something in the air, an awareness akin to the stillness before a storm.

"I have a grandson, don't I?"

Nathan let his fork drop the short distance to his plate, and he pushed it all away. He couldn't meet his mother's eyes, wasn't sure he wanted to know what she thought of him and this situation.

"Yes, but don't say anything. Grace wants to…keep it quiet for now."

"Not tell him?"

He still didn't agree with Grace and part of him wanted to scream at her, but he found himself hiding those feelings from his mother. "She's afraid he's too young."

"I don't understand. Why bring him here then?"

He lost the fight and let his eyes drift toward Grace and Evan again. "She wants to make sure Evan has somewhere to go if anything ever happens to her. And she doesn't want him going to her family."

"She's broken away from them?"

"More like they tossed her out on her butt."

"That's sad."

He watched Grace and tried to put himself in her teenage shoes. Imagined how frightened she'd been that day, standing on her parents' porch, knowing she was totally on her own with nothing. "It's more than sad. She's been through a lot."

"And yet you're mad at her."

"Yes."

"Understandable, on both sides."

He glanced at his mother then, and she met his gaze.

"Her family was a real piece of work," she said. "I hate that she was hurt in the process, but I'm glad she's free of them."

"She said it felt like they'd brainwashed her."

"Of that I have no doubt."

"They made her afraid to tell me." Of course, his actions hadn't helped matters any, but he couldn't tell his mother how big of an ass he'd been in the days after he'd gotten a bit too tipsy at Blake Chester's party and taken Grace to bed.

"Then you'll just have to convince her there's nothing to be afraid of."

"Easier said than done."

"Things worth having are rarely easy."

A few more silent moments passed as he tried to figure out how to approach Grace, Evan, the entire situation.

"How did you know?" he asked his mother.

"Because he looks just like you at that age."

Nathan eyed Evan, tried to see himself in the boy. And there it was—the shape of the chin, the dark blond hair so unlike Grace's bright blond waves, the way he talked to anyone who would listen. If he and his mom could see it, how long before his dad and brothers came to the same conclusion? How long before Grace's secret was out, even if he stayed quiet?

He just hoped she wouldn't blame him and take Evan away before he even got a chance to know him. He couldn't let that happen no matter what Grace wanted or what she'd been through.

He wouldn't.

Chapter Four

"Don't look now, but I think Mr. Hunky Cowboy is checking you out," Laney said as she slid back into her spot next to Grace, two slices of apple pie in hand.

Grace's skin warmed at the thought that Nathan was watching her, but then common sense took over. If he was staring at her, it likely wasn't with romantic interest. He was probably stewing in his anger or trying to figure out a way to change her mind about telling Evan about his father's identity.

"You do remember you're on my side, right?"

"I'm not talking about Nathan."

Grace glanced at Laney as her friend placed

a slice of pie in front of her. And then she noticed a man at the next table looking her way. When their gazes met, he smiled at her from below his straw cowboy hat. She managed a quick but noncommittal smile back before averting her gaze.

Laney cut off a piece of her pie. "While Evan's having fun this week, who says you can't, too?" Laney waggled her eyebrows.

Grace shook her head. "Me, that's who."

"Might be a good way to make Nathan jealous."

"I'm not here for that, either. Plus, I don't want to do anything else he can hold against me."

Laney shrugged. "Whatever. You don't have to be pure as the driven snow to be a good mother." Having said her piece, as she always managed to do, Laney took her first bite of Merline's signature apple pie. Grace hadn't tasted her own yet, but it wasn't necessary to remember the taste. Like so many things from those months when she was tutoring Nathan, slices of scrumptious apple pie stood out in her memory as if days and not years had passed.

"Oh, this is good," Laney said.

Before she slipped up and admitted a part of her actually did like the idea of Nathan being jealous, Grace took a bite of her pie and made appreciative noises.

Laney made a slight nod toward the man at the other table. "You have to admit he's nice-looking."

"He is, but the last things I need in my life right now are more complications."

"Party pooper."

Grace stared at Laney. "I should have brought Emily instead."

Laney wiped her mouth with a napkin. "I can't help it. I'm an incurable matchmaker. How many times did I try to set you up in college?"

"I'm sorry, but you're still out of luck with me. I'm firmly single and like it that way."

Most of the time. Except when she looked into Nathan's eyes and her heart performed some fancy Fred Astaire dance steps in her chest.

Laney pouted. "But I think all the other women here are married. Hot cowboys with no one to pair them with, that's a crime."

Grace laughed. "Sorry to spoil your fun."

"Hey, the week isn't over yet."

When Grace finished her pie, she gathered Laney's and her trash and headed for the large garbage can at the edge of the picnic area.

After tossing the trash inside, she turned to find the unnamed cowboy standing behind her. "Oh, excuse me."

He touched the brim of his hat. "No problem." He lifted his empty plate. "Good dinner, wasn't it?"

"Yes."

The man reached around her and deposited his own trash in the can. "Name's Barrett Farnsley, from Oklahoma City." He paused until it registered that he wanted to know her name.

"Grace Cameron." She deliberately left off where she was from.

"A very pretty name, for a very pretty lady."

Grace blushed despite herself. She'd had interest from men before, but something about being back here in this place where she'd fallen in love for the first and only time had her emotions heightened. "Thank you." She didn't know what else to say. Barrett was indeed handsome with short, dark hair just visible at the edges of his hat, and light blue eyes.

But he wasn't Nathan.

And maybe that was a good thing.

It couldn't hurt to just be friendly, could it? They'd all be gone in a week anyway.

"I assume one of these wild children is yours." She pointed toward where all the kids were playing fetch with a couple of large Labradors, one chocolate, one yellow.

"Two, actually. The twins."

"A handful?"

"To say the least."

Grace smiled. Evan was a handful all on his own. She couldn't imagine having to wrangle two boys the same age.

Barrett shoved his hands into his back pockets. "Are you here with anyone?"

Subtle. "Just my son. He's the one who looks like he's determined to ride the dog."

Barrett laughed, and she had to admit it was a nice laugh. Big, full, uninhibited. If she weren't so tied in emotional knots right now, if all her focus wasn't on Evan's future, she might actually be tempted to see where things went with Barrett. If anywhere. She was so bad at reading men's signals that she could have what she thought was Barrett's interest totally wrong. After all, she'd once thought that Nathan cared about her.

He'd just been like every other teenage boy, interested only about getting in a girl's pants.

She made the mistake of looking toward where she'd seen him sitting next to his mother earlier. He was watching her, and he didn't look happy. For the tiniest of moments, she did hope he wore that look because he was jealous.

Grace reminded herself she wasn't at the ranch to rekindle things with Nathan. Bad idea, very bad idea. She was simply falling victim to some old wishful thinking. Nathan no doubt wore that unfriendly expression because he was still angry with her and this situation she'd thrust upon him.

A squeal of panic jerked her attention toward the kids. One of the dogs had a little girl down on her back. Parents vacated their tables and conversations and hurried toward the children. Grace got there first and grabbed the dog by the collar. "Choco, no!" She tugged the dog off the little girl.

The child's mother scooped her up and turned angry eyes toward the Teagues. "How could you let an animal like this near our children?"

Grace touched the woman's arm, spoke to her in a soothing, mother-to-mother tone. "She's okay. See, no injuries. Choco was just kissing her, being friendly."

The woman examined her daughter to see for herself, then pulled her close and headed out of the picnic area without another word.

"Why is that lady mad?" Evan asked from beside Grace.

She wrapped her arm around his waist. "She was just scared, afraid her daughter was hurt."

"How did you know Choco's name?"

She hadn't even thought about it, just identified the dog because she'd known it from when he was a puppy. "I heard someone call him earlier." She hated lying to her son, but the truth might lead to too many questions she wasn't ready to answer.

She stood and dusted off her hands. "I think it's time we called it a night, squirt."

"Not yet."

"Yes. If you don't get enough sleep, you won't get up in time for all the fun stuff tomorrow. You don't want to miss anything, do you?"

"No." He said it reluctantly, enough to make her smile.

She looked up from tousling his hair to find herself facing Nathan. Her heart thumped hard, part fear, part an ill-advised thrill at being near him.

"Thanks for that," he said.

"What?"

"Jumping into the dog fray."

She shrugged. "No problem. I could tell

what Choco was doing." She glanced down at Evan, hoping he didn't pick up on anything too familiar between her and Nathan.

Nathan propped his hands on his hips. "I'm guessing we'll lose another guest tonight though."

"Maybe not. She probably just needs time to calm down. We moms tend to overreact sometimes."

Nathan's gaze shifted to Evan, and she had to fight the burning need to hurry Evan away. And her guilt at feeling that way.

Evan looked up at Nathan. "Do we get to ride tomorrow?"

Nathan hesitated just long enough to increase Grace's nervousness even more. "If you're very good and do what your mother says."

Evan thought about this for a moment, then nodded. "Mom, I need to go to bed."

She bit her lip to keep from smiling at Evan's quick about-face. And she tried to ignore the twinge of annoyance that he was so much quicker to agree with Nathan than her, even without the knowledge Nathan was his father. Maybe it was just a guy thing, a boy responding to a male authority figure, something Evan had never had but innately listened to. She couldn't say that made her particularly happy.

Past Nathan's shoulder, she noticed Merline watching them. "Evan, go wait in the car. I'll be there in a minute." When he was out of hearing range and the rest of the dog-incident spectators had wandered away, she looked at Nathan. "Your mom knows, doesn't she?"

"She figured it out on her own. I haven't told anyone."

"Will she tell the others?"

"Dad, maybe. They don't keep secrets from each other."

"Nathan—"

"Don't worry. No one will say anything to Evan. Not yet."

She wanted assurances, long-term, but she didn't push it. The fatigue she'd been feeling all day was winning, and she needed to be more rested before she went toe-to-toe with Nathan or any of the Teagues.

But as she lay in bed two hours later, staring at the ceiling and listening to Evan's breathing in the other bedroom, she wondered if she'd get any rest the entire week. And if she did fall asleep, would Nathan follow her into her dreams?

* * *

It might technically be a vacation in the sense that she didn't have to go to the office, but there would be no luxurious sleeping in. Not when Evan was so anxious to get back to playing cowboy. Grace heaved herself out of bed, feeling a bit like she'd been dragged behind one of the ranch's horses. As she made her way toward the bathroom, she answered her own question from the sleepless hours the night before. Yes, Nathan Teague had followed her into her dreams.

At some point, she'd finally fallen asleep, but it hadn't been the restful kind. Bits and pieces of the dreams floated to the surface of her brain as she started the shower running and stripped off her pajamas.

Nathan yelling at her. Nathan grabbing Evan and running down a dark alley where she couldn't follow. Nathan taking her in his arms and kissing her like it was the end of time and they only had a few moments to live.

"Mom! Can I have a muffin?"

Grace jumped at the sound of Evan's voice through the bathroom door, as if he could see the images running through her head. "Have you brushed your teeth?"

"Yes."

"Then have a muffin and some juice. Watch TV until I get ready."

"Okay, but hurry. We're going to ride today."

"Yes, I remember."

She stepped into the shower and tried to wash the memories of all the dreams down the drain. Attempting to focus on other things, she made a mental checklist for her day. Take Evan to the barn. Check in with Emily. Sketch out some ideas for the Franklin Mountain Lodge proposal. Stop thinking about how Nathan's hands had felt on her body in the dream she was having just before Evan woke her up.

She shoved her face below the rush of water and turned down the temperature. After a few more minutes, she shut off the water and stood dripping. Coming back to Blue Falls was so much harder than she'd thought. How had she convinced herself that those teenage feelings she'd harbored for Nathan were gone? More like they'd just gone dormant until she'd seen him again, a grown-up Nathan who was even more attractive than he'd been the one time he'd held her.

"Mom! Are you ready?"

Grace shook her head and reached for a towel. "Almost."

Which was a lie. She was nowhere near ready to face Nathan Teague again.

Nathan got the little girl named Cheyenne—who was dressed in pink yet again today, this time pink-and-white checks on her shirt with those pink boots and hat—settled on the horse. "That's good. You're a natural."

"Thank you." She smiled so wide, so full of youthful joy, that he couldn't help smiling back.

Something about her, maybe the blond pigtails, reminded him of Grace. But something told him that she'd never been this happy as a child. Well, that wasn't his fault, was it? His thoughts and feelings toward her twisted in knots. How could he be so angry with her and feel sorry for her at the same time? He liked his life simple, and she was making it all kinds of complicated.

He handed off Cheyenne and her mount to his father and turned with a sigh to see who was next. Instead of the next in a line of kids, he spotted his older brother leaning against the fence.

"You sure are a grump this morning," Simon said.

"Bite me."

"Nathan, the children." The sarcasm oozed from his words.

"Don't you have someone to go arrest?" In addition to being in charge of the ranch maintenance, Simon served as the local sheriff.

"Maybe you, for biting off heads."

Nathan forced himself to stop grinding his teeth. How was he going to make it through an entire week of having to watch his son without being able to tell him he was his father? And what right did Grace have to ask it of him? None.

This was not about how the father of those rowdy twins had been ogling her. Really, it wasn't.

"So, this got anything to do with Grace Cameron coming back to town?"

"No."

"Yeah, that's what I thought. I'm guessing she's not back for old times' sake, either."

Nathan ventured a look at his brother and found him watching Evan as he rubbed his little hand down Dolly's mane from his perch in the saddle. Man, he looked so small up there, and Nathan battled the unexpected urge to rush to Evan's side, to make sure he didn't fall off and hurt himself. He sighed again, all too aware that his brother had figured out the truth, as well. Not much got past Simon. It's what made him a good sheriff.

"Don't say anything." If anyone said anything, it was going to be him.

"Not my place." A few moments passed before Simon spoke again. "What are you going to do?"

"I don't know. Still haven't gotten used to the idea yet."

"Does the boy know?"

"No, and Grace asked me to keep it that way."

"And you're going along with that? You're either a better man or a bigger fool than I am."

"I plan to change her mind before she leaves."

"So she's not staying?"

"That's what she says. She has a business in Arkansas."

Simon lifted his hat and resettled it on his head. "Hope you're not planning to win her over with that sunny personality you've been wearing since yesterday."

"I'd like to see you act any better in this situation."

"Point taken. Still, you've got powerful little time to work with here." Simon shoved away from the fence. "Well, I'll go see if I can find someone to arrest."

Nathan considered his brother's words as he listened to Simon's truck start and head down the driveway. He hated to admit it, but Simon was right. His sour attitude wasn't going to convince Grace that he should be a part of Evan's life. Surely he could manage reining in his anger if it meant having a relationship with his son. Didn't mean it was going away, but he could pretend for the bigger cause.

Once he made the decision to try to be less of a standoffish jerk, he was chomping at the bit to get at it. But Grace stayed out of the corral as he, his dad and their two best hands, Abel and Juan, took the kids through short rides and lessons about how to handle horses.

He tried not to be obvious about snatching glances at her where she sat on that same bench she'd sat on the day before when she'd told him Evan was his son. Still, his dad caught him a couple of times. The way he creased his forehead made Nathan think his mother hadn't shared the news about Evan yet. But it was only a matter of time.

When the morning session concluded, he inhaled a deep breath and approached Evan. "You did well this morning. You'll be riding the range before you know it."

"Really?"

"Well, maybe a few years down the road, but you seem to have a way with horses." It was the truth. None of the horses seemed to spook around him, and Dolly was already acting as though Evan was her best friend.

Nathan turned at the sound of someone hurrying toward him. His eyes met Grace's, and he saw the fear there that he was going back on his word. His jaw tightened before he told himself to relax.

Grace shifted her attention to Evan. "How'd it go, cowboy?"

"Great! Nathan says I'll be riding the range soon."

"I think I said in a few years." Before he thought, he reached out and squeezed Evan's shoulder. The realization that he was touching his son for the first time sent a jolt through him, enough to make him take a step back.

"Go wash your hands," Grace said. "There's a sink inside the barn."

"Okay. I'm starving." Evan ran toward the barn, fueled by boundless energy.

"Nathan."

It took a moment for Grace's voice to filter through the roaring in his head. "Yeah?"

"Are you okay?"

He looked toward the barn entrance, could

just make out Evan inside the dim interior. "I know this sounds insane, but it was like it all wasn't real until I touched him."

"Did you…say anything?"

"No."

"Thank you."

Nathan redirected his attention back to the woman who'd had his child. His *child.* He choked down the feeling of betrayal that ate at him. "I'm going to change your mind, Grace."

She started to shake her head, but he grabbed her hand, squeezed it gently.

"I've got a week. I *will* change your mind."

Chapter Five

The truth Grace had settled on the night before remained the same the next morning.

She had to stay away from Nathan. Otherwise, she feared his promise would come true. He'd change her mind.

And she'd risk losing Evan.

But that didn't feel true anymore, did it?

Maybe she was afraid of losing herself instead. Her heart. Just like she had when he'd been a heartthrob football player who needed help with the quadratic formula and she'd been the plainest of Janes.

To keep her gaze from wandering to where he stood in the corral again, she pulled out her cell phone and dialed Emily's number. As the phone rang, she glanced around and spotted Nathan instantly. Her heart squeezed in her chest when she noticed him laughing with Evan. Father and son, the two most beautiful beings in her life.

"Hello?" Emily sounded out of sorts, drawing Grace's attention away from the scene.

"What's wrong?"

"Oh, hey. Didn't realize it was you."

"Okay, we have this thing called Caller ID."

"And I'm dealing with this thing called a paper jam. I'm about to have an *Office Space* moment."

"Please don't beat the copier to death. We can't afford another one right now."

"Why do you always have to make sense?"

"I'm the smart one?"

"Ha!" Emily cursed under her breath, calling the hinky copier a few choice terms. "So, how's it going there?"

"Okay, so far."

"How did Nathan take the news?"

She watched the man in question as he led Evan around the corral, her little cowboy having the time of his life. "About like I expected. Disbelief, confusion. No small amount of anger."

"Did he agree to not say anything to Evan?"

"For the time being, but he's determined to change my mind before I leave."

"And you're afraid he might?"

"No." She watched the way Nathan moved, remembered how he'd moved with her that long-ago night, how he'd moved in her dream that morning. All fluid and powerful. "Maybe."

"You want me to come down there and back up Laney for moral support, keep you strong?"

Grace shook her head as if Emily could see her. "No. One of us needs to hold down the fort."

"I'll gladly give you copier duty in exchange for hot cowboys."

"You and a cowboy? Right." Grace chuckled at the thought. "I can just imagine you discussing textiles and the merits of natural lighting with a cowboy."

"I didn't say I'd be conversing with said cowboy. And I think you're underestimating how much I hate this copier."

"Tell you what—if we land this lodge deal, we'll go crazy and buy a new one."

"You better be designing your butt off, then."

"Hey, I'm on vacation." Granted, the world's most stressful vacation.

"And I know you. I bet you have a sketch book in front of you right now."

Grace looked down at the rough drawings and notes about fabrics and furniture styles. "Guilty as charged."

"One of these days you need to take a real vacation."

"Someday."

"Is the work at least taking your mind off things?" Emily asked, more seriously.

"Not as much as I'd like. I know I did the right thing, but part of me is still afraid."

"Is Nathan how you remember him?"

"Yes, and no. I'm still sorting out what was real, what I made up in my teenage fantasies, and what was a product of what my parents told me." Other than Nathan, the officials who'd helped her get Evan back, and Laney, Emily was the only other person she'd ever told about her family.

"I know this is a cliché, but it's a good one. Just take it a day at a time. And make sure you get enough rest."

Leave it to Emily to know she'd not been sleeping well in weeks, since she'd made the decision to tell Nathan the truth. "Sometimes it's annoying how you know me so well."

"I wouldn't be doing my job as best friend if I didn't annoy you on a regular basis."

"Okay, I'm going now. I have some cowboys to ogle." Grace hung up on Emily's faux outrage, a smile on her face. That's what she'd needed—a dose of home, of familiarity, of someone she didn't have to second-guess.

When she looked up some time later, the corrals were empty. A glance at her watch showed that the morning session had already passed. She'd spent more time working than she'd realized. Her stomach growled as if to reiterate the time.

She closed her sketchbook and made her way down toward the barn, dodging pint-size campers and their parents as they filed out in search of lunch. When she didn't see Evan or Nathan, her heart rate spiked and she hurried into the cooler interior of the barn. The earthy scents of feed, hay and horses assaulted her as she checked each stall without luck.

When she started to step into the tack room, she bumped right into Nathan. She gasped and he reached out to steady her even though she'd already gripped the edge of the door frame.

"Where's Evan?"

Nathan released her and stepped to the side, his expression hardening almost imperceptibly, as if he were trying to hide his true feelings. "Right here. I was showing him how we put away the tack."

Evan walked up beside Nathan, stood next to him and emulated how his new hero stood. She couldn't let him get so attached, even if he didn't know Nathan was his father. She motioned for Evan to come to her.

"Come on, let's let Mr. Teague get to his lunch."

"Why don't you two join us up at the house?"

Right in the middle of Evan's family, where he could see photos of his father as a boy, where someone might let too much information slip.

"Thanks, but we already have plans."

"You do?" Nathan asked at the same moment Evan asked, "We do?"

"Yes, I wanted to show Evan a bit of the town, have lunch at the Primrose. I assume they still have the best country-fried steak in the Hill Country."

Nathan opened his mouth, no doubt to voice an objection, but his father interrupted by calling him from the other end of the barn. As she met Nathan's eyes, she saw the moment he decided not to press the issue. Still, he reached over and tapped the edge of Evan's hat.

"I'll see you at the roping lessons this afternoon."

Nathan met Grace's gaze for another suspended moment before he exited the tack room. Only then did she exhale in relief.

"Are you okay, Mom?"

She looked down and saw a too-familiar worry that shouldn't be in a six-year-old's eyes. He was young, but not so young that he didn't understand how very sick she'd been. When she'd been at her sickest, he'd refused to sleep in his own bed, saying he had to stay with her to make sure she was safe—as if he could battle the cancer for her.

"I'm fine, just hungry. I'm going to take you to the best place in town."

A place free of the confusing presence of Nathan Teague.

When she'd used lunch at the Primrose Café as an excuse to get away from Nathan, Grace hadn't considered the inevitable crowd. The Primrose was always busy with locals alone. Add in the tourists in town for the wildflower tours, and it was busting at the seams. As she maneuvered Evan and herself through the crowd waiting for tables, her eyes met Barrett's. He smiled and stood, edging his way toward her.

Too late to leave now.

Now she regretted not accepting Laney's invitation to go shopping with her and Cheyenne.

"Grace, if I'd known you were coming here, we could have all ridden together."

"It was a last-minute decision."

"Well, I'm glad you made it. Come sit with us."

"Oh, no, we'll wait our turn."

"Mom, we're going to be late for the roping." When had her child gotten so whiny?

"Really, we have plenty of room," Barrett said.

Grace couldn't refuse again without being deliberately rude, so she nodded and steered Evan through the maze of packed tables. When he reached the table, he launched right into a conversation with Barrett's sons, ignoring her completely. Her boy—never met a stranger.

"Boys, this is Ms. Cameron. Grace, this is Tyler and Jason."

"Nice to meet you," she said.

The two tow-headed boys nodded and went right back to debating with Evan over who was going to get the Cowboy Camper award at the end of the week. Posturing and testosterone already at work at such a young age.

"Maybe one of the girls will win," she said.

Evan seemed to consider the possibility, but the twins made similar faces that showed their abject horror at the idea. "It's a cow*boy* award," Tyler said, as if she were dense.

"Manners," Barrett warned.

"Yes, sir," Tyler replied, though he didn't seem particularly thrilled about it.

"You'd think living with their mother most of the time would make them a little less like Neanderthals."

Grace smiled, unable to not like this man. "Just boys being boys."

After the waitress came and took their orders, the boys started taking turns playing a treasure-hunting game on a hand-held gaming device. They seemed to derive great satisfaction in poking fun at each other when one of their characters lost one of his virtual lives.

Grace let her gaze wander around the restaurant. She didn't recognize anyone else, but the place hadn't changed much. The walls were still covered with a jumble of photos of wildflowers, cowboys and ranches. A line of weathered older men sat on stools along the bar at the front, drinking coffee and talking about the weather and politics. Tourists gorged themselves on Texas-size meals while they read tour brochures.

"Are you two having a good vacation?" Barrett asked, drawing her attention back to their table.

"Yes, Evan is having a ball."

"How about you?"

She wasn't certain where Barrett was going with his line of questioning, but instinct told her to tread carefully. He seemed like a nice man, was attractive, but she wasn't in the market for a man. Her life was complicated enough without adding a romantic relationship to the mix—and a temporary or long-distance one at that. Maybe someday, when Evan was older, but not now. Not until she'd provided for Evan and she was more sure the cancer was gone for good.

"It's a nice place, peaceful."

Throughout the meal, Grace managed to answer questions so that they didn't reveal too much or give Barrett false hope. And in an odd way, she was sorry, because the more she got to know him, the more she realized he'd be a good catch—for someone else. Too bad he lived in Oklahoma, or she'd set him up with Emily. After all, he owned a construction company. He could build the houses, and Emily could decorate them.

Barrett sat back after finishing his meal, a satisfied look on his face. "I can see why this place is so popular. Can't remember the last time I was this full."

"Did you eat here when you were a kid?" Evan asked, catching her off guard.

"You're from here?" Barrett asked.

She answered Evan first, that yes she'd eaten here a few times, before turning to Barrett. "My family lived here for a while when I was younger." *Please don't ask anything else.*

"Then you'd be the perfect tour guide."

"What?"

Barrett patted his flat stomach. "I think after that meal, we could all use a walk around town."

Grace felt like she was being drawn further and further into a web. "We really need to get back."

"We've still got plenty of time before the afternoon activities." He eyed the boys. "There might be ice cream involved."

The chorus of excitement from the kids erased any further protest on her part. She didn't want to be the mean, no-ice-cream mom, especially not on vacation. Though she and

Evan were going to have a conversation about not getting everything they wanted.

Suspecting that Barrett might try to pay for their meals, Grace made sure she reached the cash register first. She'd already handed over her credit card by the time Barrett had wrangled his boys toward the front of the café.

"I was going to treat you to lunch," he said when he stepped up next to her.

"I wouldn't dream of it, not when you have two black holes to feed."

Barrett laughed, and she was struck again by the pleasant sound.

"Spoken like the mom of a little walking appetite of her own."

Over the next several minutes, Grace played tour guide, showing Barrett and three woefully uninterested boys the highlights of Blue Falls. She showed them the Sunday houses used by early German settlers when they came into town from their ranches on the weekends, various shops, the wonderful-smelling Mehlerhaus Bakery and Blue Falls's favorite watering hole, the Frothy Stein. How her parents had despised the bar's very existence.

As she passed the office for Wildflower Tours, she grabbed a brochure from the rack outside. Maybe she and Evan could have a little botany lesson later.

When they reached the path that made a U around three sides of the lake, Barrett made good on his promise of ice cream. She tried to decline any for herself, but he insisted.

"What is a vacation without a little splurging?" The way he looked at her, she suspected he was talking about much more than ice cream.

Feeling a strange combination of uncomfortable and flattered, she stepped up to the ice cream stand's window and ordered a scoop of black cherry.

As they made their way back toward the Primrose on the opposite side of the street, Grace resumed her duties as tour guide. When they approached the Blue Falls Music Hall, she gave a few tidbits of its history.

"The music hall in Gruene is the oldest in Texas, but this one isn't far behind. It's been fixed up a lot since I moved away." Whoever had done the renovations had made sure to keep the rustic clapboard frontier feel, though.

"Care to give us a tour of the inside?"

What she wanted was to sink into the protected confines of her car where she didn't have to worry about how to fend off advances that were nice but still felt wrong somehow. Maybe because this trip was for Evan, not her.

Not because of Nathan.

"Afraid I'm no help there. Never been inside."

"Then it'll be an adventure for all of us," Barrett said as he opened the door and stepped inside.

When the boys barreled in after him, Grace had little choice but to follow in their adventure-seeking wake. She couldn't believe how much the inside matched how she'd imagined it. Tall ceilings with rafters, wooden floor, posters on the walls advertising some of the big names and not-so-big who had played there. A long, plain bar lined one wall, and round tables sat scattered around the edges of the huge, polished dance floor. At the opposite end of the building stood the hall's famous stage, complete with old-style microphones.

Barrett, obviously reverting back to his own boyhood, rushed onto the stage and started attempting to sing a Tim McGraw song into the unplugged microphone. Evan and the twins, getting into the spirit, scrambled onto the stage and pretended to play invisible guitars and drums.

Grace laughed at their antics, which only made them goof off even more.

"I don't think they have a future on *American Idol.*"

Grace started at the sound of Nathan's voice close to her, the way it still managed to make her skin tingle. When she looked at him, she couldn't read his expression. "What are you doing here?"

He hesitated for a moment, continuing to stare toward the stage, then lifted a guitar case. "Dropping off equipment for tonight."

"Tonight?"

"Yeah. The band that was supposed to play cancelled, so we're filling in."

She glanced back at the sound of the front door opening. In stepped Ryan and Simon, the latter in a sheriff's uniform, carrying the pieces of a drum kit.

"You're in a band?"

"Yes, the Teagues of Texas."

She couldn't help but shoot him an amused smiled. "Original."

"We were going to go with Three Dudes with No Talent, but it lacked a certain ring to it."

"Ya think?" She didn't fool herself by thinking all was suddenly well between them, but even a smidge of a thaw was welcome. Even if it might be part of his plan to change her mind about telling Evan the truth.

"Hey, Grace," Simon said as he and Ryan walked by. Ryan just nodded, always the quietest of the three Teague brothers.

"So Simon is a cop now?"

"Sheriff, actually."

She laughed. "This from the boy who put honey in Coach Sanders's gym shoes?"

"Oh, that was me."

Grace noticed Nathan's mischievous smile and laughed again. "And you let him take the fall for it?"

"He loved the status it gave him."

"And this is the man protecting the good folks of Blue Falls. Good thing it's not a hotbed of crime."

"Looks like our karaoke session is over," Barrett said as he approached them, stepping a bit too close to Grace.

Grace eased a step away, trying not to be obvious and hoping she wasn't about to be in the middle of some stupid testosterone battle. But that made no sense. Nathan wasn't interested in her. But was he now the type of man who would make her think he was interested in order to convince her to tell Evan that Nathan was his father? How well had she ever really known him anyway? She examined his face as he watched Barrett. The easy expression he naturally wore was gone, replaced by a slight tightening of his jaw and an assessing look in his eyes. Did he think Barrett posed a threat to Evan?

"Well, we need to be getting back to the ranch," she said. "Evan will never forgive me if he misses the roping." No matter that the man who'd be giving the lessons stood next to her.

Her interruption of the staring contest edged things back into motion, and Barrett turned to call his boys from where they stood laughing at the clothes and hair in a seventies-era poster of Conway Twitty. Her eyes met Nathan's, and the intensity there shocked her. She looked away before she could identify its source or meaning. All she knew was that the air inside the Blue Falls Music Hall had grown too warm and she wasn't sure the extra heat wasn't coming from her.

Chapter Six

Nathan became aware that he was still standing in the middle of the empty dance floor when he looked up and saw his brothers staring at him from the stage. Not wanting questions he was pretty sure he couldn't answer, he headed for the stage steps.

"You okay?" Simon asked as he put a cymbal on a stand.

"Fine." Except for the way all his muscles had tightened and his gut had knotted when he'd seen Grace with Barrett Farnsley, laughing at his comedy routine. He'd had the irrational desire to strangle the man.

"Can't say that's convincing," Simon said. "Did you think that was convincing, Ry?"

"Nope."

"I don't recall asking you two for your expert opinions."

Simon lifted his hands in surrender. "Just making conversation."

"How about we just do this sound check. I've got to teach some kids about roping."

"One of those kids know you're his daddy yet?"

Nathan slammed down his guitar case. "Damn it, Simon. Why do you always have to dig?"

Simon shrugged. "It's what I do."

"Well, stop it."

"The boy is really yours?" Ryan asked.

Nathan met his younger brother's gaze. "Yes."

"How the hell did that happen anyway?" Simon asked. "I don't remember Grace being your kind of girl."

"And what kind was that?"

"Beautiful, not really in contention for valedictorian."

"You saying I just went for the dumb blondes?"

"Mostly, yeah. Though you obviously went for a smart one somewhere along the way."

Nathan rubbed his hand over his face. "It

was a mistake. I think I mentioned she should drop by one of Blake Chester's parties. Didn't think she'd actually do it. I'd been drinking a bit, one thing led to another."

"But—Grace Cameron?"

For some reason, Simon's disbelief rubbed Nathan the wrong way.

"She had a thing for Nathan," Ryan said. "And because of her, he got to play football."

Simon eyed Nathan. "So, it was a pity thing?"

"No!" Nathan took a few steps toward the edge of the stage, as if he could clear the fog that had clouded his brain that long-ago night. "It was…just a mistake." Why did something feel wrong when he said that? It *had* been a mistake, one brought about by stupidity and carelessness on his part. Maybe it felt wrong because it made Grace seem easily tossed away. He hadn't had a thing for her back then, but he hadn't thought of her as disposable, either. She'd been a nice, quiet girl who'd helped him.

And he'd repaid her by getting her pregnant, which led to the hardest years of her life and her nearly losing their son. Yeah, he was a real winner.

But she'd made mistakes, too, he reminded himself. Two wrongs didn't make a right.

"Is that why she moved away?" Ryan asked.

Nathan didn't know if his younger brother meant her pregnancy or the way he'd treated Grace after the night he'd had sex with her, but it didn't matter. The answer was the same, either way.

"Yes. Her parents made her."

"And you didn't know about the baby?"

Nathan shook his head. "Not until she showed up here two days ago."

"Man," Simon said. "Talk about out of left field."

"She had her reasons for not telling me, or Evan."

"Grace hasn't told Evan about you?" Ryan asked.

Nathan met Ryan's eyes. "No, and we're keeping it that way for now."

"You're okay with that?"

"I didn't say that."

"You're going to try to change her mind." Ryan nodded his approval.

"*Try* being the operative word. She's a lot more determined than she used to be."

"Dust off the old charm," Simon said.

"That's what got me into this situation in the first place."

* * *

"I'm going to have to warn the neighbors' cattle about you," Nathan said when Evan managed to rope a miniature steer dummy in the middle of the corral.

Evan beamed and looked over to where Grace stood leaning on the outside of the fence. "Did you hear that, Mom? Cows fear me."

Grace snorted as she laughed. Sometimes the funniest things came out of kids' mouths. "I heard." Her gaze shifted to Nathan, who was watching her without even attempting to hide it. She tried not to read too much into it. She'd made that mistake with him once before and didn't intend to repeat it.

Chances were everything he said and did from now on would be in the pursuit of convincing her to tell Evan the truth. She'd have to watch Nathan closely, making sure he didn't get tired of waiting and tell Evan himself. Her heart jolted at the thought. She was walking a skinny tightrope here.

"So, you here to watch your little roping prodigy or his teacher?" A good amount of teasing filled Laney's low voice.

"Evan, of course."

"Uh-huh." She didn't sound at all convinced.

At least she wasn't broadcasting it to the rest of the ranch.

"If I didn't know better, I'd swear you and Emily were twins."

Laney looked over at Grace, her eyebrows raised. "She can pick out the obvious, too?"

Grace turned her back on the activities in the corral, on Nathan. "Am I really that obvious?"

"If they plunked the Statue of Liberty in the middle of this ranch, it couldn't be more obvious that you're still attracted to him, no matter how nervous he makes you."

"Damn it." How could she have let those old feelings surface? Because that's what they had to be, right? Remnants of unresolved and unrequited longing from the past.

"If it helps any, I'd say it goes both ways."

"Now that's where you're wrong."

"I'm pretty good at reading people."

Grace was already shaking her head. "Trust me. I'm not what Nathan is interested in."

Laney angled herself toward Grace. "And you know this how?"

"Because he told me to my face that he was going to change my mind about telling Evan the truth. Anything he says or does is suspect."

"You're smart enough to know the difference between genuine interest and ulterior motive."

"I'm not so sure about that. I wouldn't say I have the best track record with judging Nathan's feelings. Would you?"

Laughter filled the air behind Grace. She looked back to see Tyler had missed the steer but had roped his brother instead.

"You're not that starry-eyed, naive girl anymore, Grace. If he's trying to play you for a fool, you'll know." Laney propped her forearms on the fence. "And then I'll be forced to make good on my earlier offer to kick his jeans-clad butt all the way to the Mexican border and back. You might owe me a pair of new shoes by the time I'm done."

Grace hated how her heart constricted at the memory of the hurt she'd experienced when he'd ignored her after the most important night of her life.

"I know you don't think he liked you back then, but there are definitely sparks now. Maybe he's changed as much as you have. Nobody ever said teenage boys weren't stupid, but they do eventually grow up."

Grace's pulse jumped at the very idea that Nathan might be interested in her, really interested. But that was dangerous thinking.

I'm going to change your mind.

Would he really stoop to playing with her past feelings for him? She'd confessed to him that she'd liked him when she'd been his tutor, after all. She didn't want to think he would use those old feelings to his advantage now, but she hadn't wanted to admit she'd been nothing more than an alcohol-induced roll in the hay, either.

She'd come a long way in trusting people since he'd ignored her and her parents had tossed her out, but she suspected the tendency toward distrust, to never put her faith fully in anyone but herself, might stay with her throughout her entire life.

"Just be open to the possibility," Laney said. "That's all I'm saying."

Grace nodded but told herself not to bank on it.

"Girls can do anything boys can." Cheyenne's voice rose above all the other conversations.

Grace looked toward where Cheyenne was faced off against Evan, Tyler, Jason and another little boy Grace thought was named Andy, her small hands on her hips.

"Uh-oh. Those boys taunted the wrong girl," Laney said.

"We could win a contest against girls anytime," Tyler said, eyeing Cheyenne as well as Meaghan and Becca, the only other girls among the campers.

Grace looked around for Barrett, but he'd vacated the spot where he'd been talking to a couple of the ranch hands.

Nathan waded into the fray. "Well, that doesn't seem fair since there are more of you guys than girls. Unless we can convince one of you ladies to join the girls' side." Nathan stared directly at Grace, a glint of challenge and a poorly hidden smile in his expression.

Her breath caught, and she called herself a fool for letting what might be a well-calculated smile get to her so easily.

"Like I said," Laney said under her breath. "Sparks."

Ignoring the sudden fluttering of her heart, Grace climbed over the fence and made her way across the packed dirt as if she were a gladiator entering the arena. She wouldn't let Nathan know how drawing closer to him made her senses go haywire. She was simply showing solidarity with the girls.

"Looks like we've got ourselves a full team," Nathan said, sounding so amused she wanted to smack him on the arm.

Oh, how easy it would be to just give in and enjoy her time with him, pretending it might mean more than it actually did, no matter how much it might hurt her later.

But maybe that was the best tactic for handling her situation—to quit fighting it so hard. To go along on the surface while doing her best to guard the part of her heart Nathan was uniquely qualified to break.

"You can just wipe that smirk off your face, Nathan Teague."

"Yes, ma'am." He tipped the edge of his hat, and again her heart did that ill-advised flippy thing. "Okay, we'll take turns, and each person gets three tries. The team with the most successful attempts wins."

Grace took up her position behind the little girls, noticing her son snickering right along with the other boys. She rolled her eyes at the silliness of boys, no matter their age. Once the snickering faded, Nathan handed the lariat to Tyler with some helpful reminders about what he'd been teaching them.

Tyler nailed his first try, then pumped his fist and said, "Yes!"

Cheyenne didn't let him get to her and responded with a successful throw of her own.

"Way to go, Chey!" Laney said from her post on the sidelines.

Cheyenne didn't celebrate as visibly as Tyler, just returned to her team with a smug smile on her face. Grace gave her a high five anyway. All the other kids, including Evan, missed their throws, leaving Grace facing her turn. She stared at the miniature steer dummy and wondered, how hard could this be?

"Nervous?" Nathan asked as he handed her the coiled rope.

"Nope."

He smiled, a reaction so at odds with how he'd acted toward her since her revelation that it made her suspicious. Still, she was going to play along.

"You become a cowgirl since I last saw you?" he asked, sounding skeptical.

She had the distinct urge to stick her tongue out at him, and suspected he knew it. As she stepped forward, she replayed every tip she'd heard Nathan tell the kids. She swirled the rope with visions of saving the day for womankind. As she let the rope fly, she held her breath—right until it fell flat in the dirt.

Tyler and his cohorts started guffawing. Despite his budding male chauvinism—something else they'd be discussing—it was good to see Evan so happy. Meaghan responded by saying, "There's two more tries, you nits."

"Now, no name calling," Nathan said. When Tyler started to smile, Nathan pointed at him and the other boys. "And no rubbing it in. This is just friendly competition. If you can't handle that, we'll quit. Can you all handle that?"

Chastised, all the kids nodded. Then Nathan looked at her with a raised eyebrow. "Grace?"

"Seriously?"

He smiled a little, like he was enjoying teasing her. Could Laney possibly be right? "You are a part of the girls' team."

She nodded then watched more carefully as he gave pointers to the boys and girls alike. Something shifted inside her when she realized how good he was with them, how his speech about friendly competition had been so…fatherly. Nathan Teague was beginning to chip away at the image she'd carried of him all the years she'd been away. Was she making a mistake not letting him be a part of Evan's life?

She shifted her attention to the small gathering that had assembled to watch the contest. Fellow campers, their parents, ranch hands. The grandparents and an uncle Evan didn't know he had. Was she, through her fear of losing him, cheating Evan? Punishing people who'd done nothing worthy of punishment?

"Are you okay?"

She jerked at the nearness of Nathan's voice. "Yeah."

He looked at her as if he was trying to work a tricky puzzle. "You were on another planet."

"Sorry. Daydreaming, I guess."

"About anything interesting?" he asked low, where no one else could hear.

The way he said it—private, just for her, in a voice that struck her as sexy—caused her nerves to spark. When she met his eyes, her breath caught in her chest. For one crazy moment, she ached to be alone with him so she could kiss that teasing expression off his too-gorgeous-for-her-peace-of-mind face. She should ignore his question, but a part of her that hadn't even existed in high school decided to give as good as she got. If he was playing her, he'd be surprised when she fired back.

She offered up a knowing smile as she accepted the rope. "Wouldn't you like to know?" Without waiting for his reaction, she took her turn and found success this time.

Whoever had temporarily inhabited her body vacated the premises as quickly as she'd arrived, leaving Grace's knees rubbery and her unable to meet Nathan's eyes as the rest of the contest played out.

Meaghan finally roped the faux steer, resulting in much jumping and squealing between her and her teammates. The girls were one up on the boys, meaning they'd won despite how Grace's last throw might go. Still, she stepped forward, concentrated, and let the rope fly. It neatly fell over the fake horns, and the girls went wild again while the boys made sounds of disbelief.

Nathan retrieved the rope and began coiling it as he walked toward her with what seemed like deliberate slowness. And she felt as though her sneakers had taken root in the Texas dirt.

"You're a woman of many talents." Again, his voice felt like a delicious assault on her senses, and she wished she could trust it. "Dancing among them?"

She stared at him. "What?"

"Dancing. You know, music, feet moving around a dance floor."

She crossed her arms. "I know what dancing is."

"But do you like it?"

She should say no, kill wherever this line of questioning was going, but she didn't. The fact was she loved dancing, something she'd never been allowed to do while growing up. "Yeah."

"Good." With no more explanation, he turned and walked away. "Congratulations to the girls' roping team. With that, we'll call it a day." He faced the assembly. "If you're looking for something to do tonight, there will be music and dancing at the Blue Falls Music Hall in town. And it's family night, which means the bar won't be serving alcohol. So bring the kids."

Grace would swear he looked directly at Evan right before his gaze caught hers. A wave of confusion rolled through her, making her wonder what to believe. Had Nathan been flirting with her because he was interested, as Laney claimed? Or was he just counting on potential lingering feelings so he could spend more time with Evan, time in which he might decide to reveal the truth and strip away her choice of how and when to tell Evan about his paternity?

An image of dragging a screaming Evan away from his newfound father shook her. Needing to get away, she headed for the group of people filing through the barn. Before she could make a clean exit, however, Nathan's long stride caught up with then passed her. He turned and walked backward for a few steps. "Save me a dance."

Hard to do if she wasn't there.

"So, what do you want to do tonight, cowboy?" Grace asked Evan as they sat on the front porch of their cabin drinking lemonade. "Movie? Go out for pizza?"

"Go to the dance."

His answer surprised her, especially considering how he always laughed when he found her dancing while cleaning the house.

"It'll be crowded and noisy." *And your father will be there.*

"Cheyenne said it'd be fun. She said cowboys are good dancers."

"She did, did she?" Where had she come up with that idea? Grace was pretty sure there was no dancing on PBR coverage.

But she was glad her discussion with her son about respecting girls had sunk in and he'd spent some time talking with Cheyenne before they'd all returned to their cabins. He'd only stopped when the Farnsley boys had started laughing at him.

"Yeah, plus Nathan's band is playing. I bet he's good. Don't you think he's probably good?"

Yeah, at many things, like winning over her son.

And making her body flush with a longing that was a very bad idea.

I just have to make it through the rest of the week. Then we'll be home, back to normal, away from the crazy pull Nathan has on me.

Why didn't that feel as appealing as it had a couple of days ago?

The door to the cabin next door opened, and Laney and Cheyenne stepped out. Cheyenne smiled and waved. "Hi, Evan."

When Grace glanced at Evan, his cheeks were flushed with embarrassment, but that didn't stop him from waving back at Cheyenne. Was it possible to have a crush in first grade? From the look on Evan's face when he thought she wasn't looking at him, she'd guess yes. Cheyenne did look cute in a white fringed skirt and pink cowgirl shirt embroidered with flowers on the lapels, but Grace wasn't ready for this. Wouldn't be ready for many more years, if ever.

"Aren't you all ready?" Laney asked.

"I'm not sure we're going. It's been a long day." Grace tried to ignore the undisguised look of disappointment on Cheyenne's face.

"Of course you're going."

"Really, I didn't bring anything to wear to a dance."

Laney walked over to the edge of the porch and grasped Grace's hand. "Lucky for you, I am physically incapable of packing light." She tugged until Grace stood and allowed herself to be escorted toward Laney's cabin. "Be ready in twenty minutes," Laney said to Evan over her shoulder.

"I need to help him."

"He'll be fine. It's his mom who needs the prodding."

As they crossed the threshold into the cabin, Grace stopped and met the other woman's eyes. "Why are you doing this?"

"Because I'm an old married lady and have to live vicariously. And I'm not about to let you rob me of my fun."

Grace must have had a comical look on her face because Laney laughed and pushed her toward the bedroom.

"You don't even know Nathan or what he might be planning," Grace said.

"Neither do you, not anymore."

Grace planted her feet and turned to stare at Laney. "Did you plan this all along?" That idea hurt, that one of her best friends might push her in a direction she wasn't prepared to go.

"No."

"Then why the change?"

"Because I see how you look at him, how Evan is already halfway to worshipping the ground Nathan walks on."

"Nathan wants nothing more than to change my mind, to have a say in a situation I've handled on my own for nearly seven years."

"Do you blame him?"

"Laney!"

"For just a moment, think of the situation from his point of view. He's been a father all these years and didn't know it."

Grace stalked across the room. "I bet Emily wouldn't be doing this right now."

Laney crossed to stand opposite Grace. "I'm going to forgive you that because I know this is hard for you."

"I can't let him take Evan from me." Grace swallowed past the lump in her throat. "I couldn't survive that."

"Do you really think that will happen?"

"I don't know, but how can I risk it?"

"How can you live the rest of Evan's childhood in fear?" Laney took Grace's hands in hers. "Listen. All I'm asking you to do is take it one step at a time, and tonight that means going to a dance. You deserve to have some fun."

Grace met Laney's eyes and could tell her friend was holding back more that she wanted to say. "What?"

"Have you considered that this could work out better than you ever hoped?"

"What do you mean?"

Laney hesitated for a moment before answering. "What if this time Nathan liked you back? Maybe you three could be a real family."

Grace shook her head. "I can't even think that."

"Why not?"

The truth clawed its way out. "Because it would hurt too much when it didn't come true."

Laney opened her mouth to say something else, but Grace held up a hand to stop her. "I'll go to the dance, maybe even enjoy it, but I can't open myself up to any more pain. I've had enough."

To her credit, Laney nodded in understanding. "Well, if you're going dancing, I'm at least going to make you look presentable."

Grace smiled. "Why do I suddenly feel like I'm on *What Not to Wear?*"

Laney just smiled and rubbed her hands together in anticipation.

Twenty minutes later, Grace stood in front of the bathroom mirror wearing a red strapless sundress and white sandals with kitten heels, her hair styled in gentle, carefree waves. Tears pooled in her eyes. She hadn't looked this good, this healthy, in a long time.

"What's wrong?" Laney's reflection showed concern.

"It's just been a while since I did anything like this."

Laney squeezed Grace's shoulders. "Do something for yourself?"

Grace edged her way out of the bathroom. "I'm just going because Evan wants to."

Laney followed her into the living room then leaned back against the couch and crossed her arms. "Do you ever do anything for you alone?"

There she was, sounding like Emily again. "Yes."

"What?"

"My business."

"Work doesn't count."

"Even if I love what I do?"

"Nope. Even if you love it, work is a means to an end—an end that probably has everything to do with providing for your son."

"And that's a bad thing?"

"Of course not. But you have to do stuff for yourself, too, especially after everything you've gone through. Think of it as a good lesson for Evan. He'll see that people can take care of others without forgetting to enjoy their own lives."

Grace took a few steps toward the window and spotted Evan and Cheyenne sitting on the steps of the other cabin. Laney was right. Evan had been able to get himself ready all on his own. Laney's footsteps caused the floorboards to squeak as she walked over to join Grace.

"Trust me on this," Laney said. "When Chey was sick, I gave everything to her, absolutely everything. So much so that when she got better, Stephen and I barely recognized each other. I couldn't remember the last time we'd slept in the same bed. One of us was always with Chey, either at the hospital or in Chey's room at home. I got her back and almost lost him."

"I'm sorry. I didn't know." Grace understood that bone-deep need to take care of her child, to do whatever it took. She admired Laney for it. But her friend had been hurting in other ways. "Why didn't you tell us?"

Laney shrugged. "You had enough on your own plate. Plus, I just wanted to make it better and pretend it never happened." She picked at the fabric on the back of the couch. "Sometimes I think about what would have happened if we'd lost Chey. Stephen and I, neither one of us would have had anyone to turn to, to grieve with. We would have both been utterly alone. Chey's illness would have killed not only her but the love we'd once shared, too."

"Are…are you two okay now?"

"It took time and hard work, but we made our way back to each other. And you know what? Because we're happy, Chey's happy."

Grace watched Evan as he pointed toward something in one of the nearby trees, a bird maybe. "And you think that's what I should do with Nathan, find my way back to him?"

Laney lifted her shoulders a fraction. "I don't know if he's your Mr. Happily Ever After, but what harm could it do to dance with the man, maybe flirt a little?"

Grace sighed and pointed out the window, at Evan. "That can happen."

Chapter Seven

As the final notes of the third song in their first set faded away, Nathan accepted that Grace and Evan weren't coming to the music hall. His stomach had been jittery all afternoon at the thought of seeing her again. He kept telling himself it was because time was ticking away, and he had to use every opportunity to change her stance on telling Evan the truth so they could avoid a potentially ugly situation. But a voice inside him kept demanding that he stop lying to himself.

Despite still being upset over her decision to keep Evan all to herself, he was attracted to Grace. Really attracted. She'd grown into a beautiful woman, and he wasn't the only man to notice. As he and his brothers launched into Toby Keith's "Should've Been a Cowboy," he noticed Barrett Farnsley still shooting the front door glances as he talked with Nathan's dad and a couple of the other campers' fathers. If there was one good thing about Grace skipping out tonight, it was that she wasn't dancing with Farnsley while Nathan had to watch from the stage.

He was in the middle of the chorus when the door opened. He'd swear his heart missed a beat, but then the crowd shifted to reveal little Cheyenne and her mom. What was wrong with him? He'd never felt this way in high school, when a person's emotions were supposed to be all wonky. Maybe he just felt bad for all she'd gone through, even admired her for everything she'd accomplished on her own—that, and the undeniable fact that she was a stunner. He had to stop thinking about her or he was going to flub the lyrics to the song and be left without a good explanation.

When he shifted his attention to his brothers and the three of them started playing off each other, the crowd got even louder. He fed off it and ended the song with a rousing flourish. They'd launched into the next song when he saw Grace. She'd slipped in while his attention had been on playing. It was a good thing Simon had the lead vocals on the current song because he was stunned speechless. Grace was simply beautiful. Even if she weren't the mother of his son, he'd want her. Her, not anything she might be able to give him.

As he just managed to get through the familiar notes, he watched her every move, not caring who saw. She looked in his direction, but the combination of the stage lights and distance kept him from being able to read her expression. But at least she was there.

His muscles tensed when he noticed Farnsley making his way toward her, much as they had when he'd seen them together that afternoon. Grace had seemed like she was having a good time, and Farnsley had made her laugh, really laugh. Did she like the man? Why else would she have been with him? And Farnsley had experience at being a father, unlike him.

His anger at having missed so much with Evan—his birth, first word, first step, first Christmas, first day of school—made a quick reappearance. His jaw tightened and he flubbed a section of the song he'd played dozens of times. Ryan managed to do a decent job of covering his mistake with an extra crash of the cymbals. Nathan refused to make eye contact with Simon.

Instead, he watched as Farnsley reached Grace and obviously asked her to dance with a gesture toward the dance floor. He gritted his teeth until Grace shook her head. Nathan couldn't help a satisfied smile as she placed her hand on Evan's shoulder.

That's right, Farnsley, back away from what's not yours.

But then Nathan's mother stepped into the picture, halting the other man's retreat.

Grace hesitated at whatever his mom had said. Surely she hadn't confronted Grace about Evan's paternity. That wasn't like her. But she'd never had a grandson on the line before. Though his mom did a better job of hiding it than he did, Nathan suspected she was upset about the lost years with Evan, too. What grandmother wouldn't be when it hit her that she'd lost all those early years of her first grandchild's life? Only when Grace allowed Farnsley to escort her to the dance floor did he realize his mother had offered to watch Evan while they danced. Why had she done that?

But Grace evidently felt safe enough to leave Evan with his grandmother. That was a positive step—even if it did come at the cost of

Nathan having to watch Grace dance with another man. It shouldn't bother him, but it did.

Focus on the positive.

Maybe Grace was already changing her mind. As they ended another song, it was all Nathan could do to not leap off the stage and ask.

"Time to slow things down a little," Simon said in advance of the next song.

Nathan shot him an ugly look, to which Simon mouthed, "What?" Nathan waved him off and settled into the slower tune. He hit another wrong note when Farnsley pulled Grace into his arms. He stared hard at the back of the man's head. But Farnsley kept dancing with Grace, and was enjoying it if the smile on his face was any indication. Nathan ground his teeth together but managed to play his part by the miracle of rote memory.

Grace glanced over Farnsley's shoulder and met Nathan's eyes for a long moment before she lowered her gaze. Could she see the intensity burning in him? Could she tell what it meant? How could she when he wasn't sure himself?

Who was he kidding? He knew exactly what it meant. He wanted to jump off the stage, march up to Farnsley and toss him aside like the interloper he was, and pull Grace close to himself instead. Very close, where he could smell her shampoo and run his fingertips over her bare shoulders, maybe trail them across all that lovely skin. He knew it didn't make sense to be angry with her and be drawn to her at the same time, but that didn't make it any less true.

When the end of the song brought the band's first scheduled break, he nearly flew off the stage as the DJ took over the music. But instead of heading for Grace, he made a beeline for the bar—only to remember as he reached it that there was no alcohol tonight. Damn, right when he needed a beer.

"What's eating you?" Simon asked before ordering a mug of root beer.

"Grace was dancing with Barrett Farnsley," Ryan answered instead.

"Oh, jealousy monster." Simon nodded like he needed no further explanation. "Well, you're free for a few. Go ask her to dance."

He almost told his brother to mind his own business, but Simon's words took hold in the part of his mind that agreed with them.

"What can I get you?" the bartender asked him.

"I'm good." At least he would be when he got Grace out of Farnsley's hands. Without a glance or word toward his brothers, he headed into the sea of dancers. He stubbornly ignored a voice in his head trying to whisper reasons why seeing Grace with Farnsley bothered him so much. That voice didn't know what it was talking about. This was lust, pure and simple. Nothing more.

And yet his heart thumped extra hard when he reached them and tapped Farnsley on the arm. "Mind if I cut in?"

For a moment, he thought the man might actually refuse. Nathan honestly didn't know how he'd respond to that. Probably not well.

"If Grace doesn't mind," Farnsley said.

Just hearing Grace's name on the man's tongue annoyed Nathan. Again, he refused to examine why.

"No, that's fine," Grace said and smiled at Farnsley.

Nathan's jaw went rigid, but he tried to hide it when Grace met his eyes.

Farnsley backed away then weaved his way through the crowd toward the bar, retracing the steps Nathan had just taken to get to Grace. Nathan didn't waste any time, placing one hand at Grace's waist and using the other to capture one of hers, hoping to erase the sight and feel of Farnsley from her memory.

Man, he was thinking like a caveman. *My woman.* Only she wasn't his, never had been.

Her hand felt so soft, so small wrapped in his. He nearly pulled away at the odd thought that his rough, callused hand might scrape that delicate skin.

They danced without speaking through an entire chorus before he felt her take a deep breath. "I don't remember you being a dancer," she said.

"What? I'm a regular Fred Astaire."

She laughed.

"You don't think so?" He spun her with a little more enthusiasm.

"I'm just surprised you know who Fred Astaire is."

"I've watched an old movie or two with my mom. My life isn't all horses and ranching."

She glanced at the stage. "No. Evidently, you're a musician now, too."

"I wouldn't say that. We just dabble, have a little fun."

"You're being too modest."

"Now there's something I've never been accused of." Was it his imagination, or did she stiffen the slightest bit? Was she remembering the stupid kid he'd been before? "I'm sorry."

She finally met his eyes then, and his breath

caught. How had he not realized how pretty her eyes were back when he'd last held her?

Because you were half-drunk, you idiot.

He noticed she was staring at him, that she must have said something. "What?"

Her eyes registered a moment of surprise then curiosity. "What are you sorry for?"

He wanted to look away but forced himself to maintain eye contact. "For how I treated you back then." Five minutes before, he'd had no thought of apologizing to her, but it felt right. No matter what she'd done in the aftermath, what he'd done to her was wrong.

She lowered her eyes so that she was probably staring at a button midway down his shirt. "Thank you."

His steps faltered. Why was she thanking him?

"It might be late, but I appreciate the apology." She cast wary glances at the people dancing nearby, as if she was afraid they all might figure out the truth and pose a threat. Then her gaze shot to where his mother and Evan sat side by side on tall stools, talking. "Your mother won't say anything, will she?"

"I asked her not to."

Grace relaxed a little. Instead of allowing

himself to get upset all over again, Nathan carefully pulled her closer.

"But she wants to know her grandson. I want to know my son."

Grace shot a suddenly panicked expression at him. He squeezed her hand, trying to reassure her, to keep her from running. "We're not going to do anything to hurt him. Or you." How was he ever going to convince her to let him into Evan's life if fear of losing Evan rode so close to the surface, just waiting to jump out and spook her?

"Family is the most important thing in the world to my mom." He had to make Grace relax so it didn't feel as though he was dancing with a very pretty, sweet-smelling tree. "That's how we got into this crazy band thing."

Her eyebrows scrunched closer together, and damned if he didn't think even her look of confusion was attractive. He fought the powerful urge to kiss away those creases on her forehead.

"Did I ever tell you about Mom's mandatory family nights?"

Grace shook her head. "We didn't talk about much other than algebra, football and horses."

Nathan winced. "Sorry."

Grace shrugged, as if the fact he'd likely

never asked her about her interests was to be expected. Little things like that made it hard to stay angry with her even though he felt he had every right.

"Every Thursday night, we all had to be home. We rotated who was in charge of family night each week. That person had to provide the meal and the entertainment."

Grace pressed her lips together then smiled. "You had to cook?"

"I said provide the meal, not cook. I used my allowance to get takeout from the Primrose when it was my turn."

"So your talents don't extend to the kitchen?" She looked on the verge of laughing.

"Only if you want people to get sick and swear off food forever."

She did laugh then, and the sound made Nathan feel as though he was standing in the sunshine. What was going on with him? Why was Grace affecting him so differently now than she had before?

Or had he always been more attracted than he'd realized? She was, after all, the first girl he'd ever made love with. All this time he'd been telling himself it was only sex, but what if he was wrong?

"So I'm guessing the band somehow made its debut on one of these family nights?"

He thought back to the scheme he and his brothers had cooked up, and how it had backfired, and laughed under his breath. "Yeah. Simon, Ryan and I had this great plan to put together a truly awful band, one so bad that our parents would forever cancel family night."

The song ended and flowed right into another. It was a faster tune, but Nathan refused to release Grace and she didn't object.

"You didn't like spending time with your parents?"

"We were teenagers. We were more interested in hanging out with our friends."

"Oh."

It hit him that his story might be giving Grace more evidence of his selfishness. She hadn't really had a loving family or friends to turn to, and he'd had both. Now that he thought of it that way, he had been selfish. He desperately wanted to make himself look better in her eyes. Maybe then she'd trust him with Evan, stop being afraid he'd take him away from her like her mother had.

"It didn't work though," he said. "Mom thought it was a great idea for us to have a band, and Dad cleaned out one of the storage buildings so we could practice."

Grace laughed, really laughed this time. "Let me guess, a building far, far away from the house."

"We have a winner." He guided her clear of another couple doing some fancy footwork. "I think they were afraid we'd scare the horses."

"More likely fear for their own eardrums."

"Hey." He tugged her closer, but what was meant to be teasing changed in an instant. Their gazes locked, and Nathan's body warmed, tingling at every point where he touched her. He splayed his hand on her lower back, loving the curves he felt there.

She tried to pull away, what he'd come to realize was a natural instinct for her, but he held fast. Not forcing, just letting her know that he didn't want her to go. It surprised him as much as it likely did her. Going so quickly from wanting to punish her to simply wanting her threatened to give him whiplash and cause him to question his sanity.

"Nathan."

He lowered his head so that he could speak into her ear. "Stop worrying. We're just dancing."

She didn't relax, but she didn't flee, either.

Instead, she allowed him to guide her around the dance floor, even offering him small smiles when their gazes connected. He had no idea what was going on between them, what the next day held, not even the rest of the night. But for the moment, holding her in his arms was enough.

Grace concentrated on keeping her heartbeat to a normal rhythm. She couldn't let Nathan know how she wanted to run and jump and scream from the rooftops how good it felt to be held in the strong circle of his arms. She had to remember that no matter who he was now, this was the man who'd hurt her, who could easily do so again. Only now there was much more at stake than her fragile feelings.

She lost track of how many songs they danced together. It was difficult to concentrate on anything other than Nathan's warm body so very close to hers, the feel of his strong hand wrapped around hers, the hardness of the muscle of his upper arm beneath the softness of his dressy black cowboy shirt.

When Ryan motioned for him to head back to the stage, Nathan hesitated. He looked down at her, and for a long moment their gazes connected and she felt as if there were words being spoken that she couldn't hear. What was he thinking? Could there be more than an ulterior motive at play here?

"Guess it's time to go entertain the masses again." He gave her a crooked grin that had her wanting to run her fingertips along his lips—lips that had once captured hers, ones she had to admit she wanted to kiss again.

She forced a casualness she didn't feel into her voice. "Can't keep your fans waiting."

He snorted out a laugh. For a moment, he looked as if he might say something more, but he just squeezed her hand and headed back toward the stage.

She'd barely taken a breath before Barrett was next to her again, ready to claim the next dance. Before he could clasp her hand, she took a step away. "I think I need a break. My feet aren't used to this."

"Shall we get a drink?"

Barrett was a nice man, really he was, but she was still caught in the afterglow of being in Nathan's arms again after so many years. It wasn't smart, she knew that, but she didn't want to ruin that feeling just yet.

"Not right now, but thank you. I need to check on Evan."

Before he could offer to accompany her, she

made her way across the crowded dance floor toward her son. As she got close, however, she saw Cheyenne tug a very unwilling-looking Evan toward the dance floor. She couldn't help but laugh as she approached Laney.

"I think your daughter is either going to run a Fortune 500 company or be president one day."

Laney nodded. "She does go after what she wants."

Grace lifted an eyebrow. "And that's my son? Thanks, but I'd like to keep him to myself a bit longer."

"Hey, he's a catch in the pre-double-digit set." Laney caught Grace's eye and nodded toward the stage. "Speaking of catches."

"It's nothing, Laney. Just a few dances." She couldn't meet her friend's eyes because she knew she couldn't hide the truth.

"You sure about that?"

In all honesty, she wasn't. When she was near Nathan, it felt as though no time had passed between the night she'd given herself to him and where they now stood. Her heart still raced, her nerves fluttered like hummingbird wings, and she wanted to believe in the impossible. Laney's words from earlier echoed in Grace's mind, tempting her to wonder if maybe it wasn't impossible anymore. After all, he'd apologized and seemed to enjoy dancing with her.

Which could all be part of his plan to change her mind about Evan.

But did that explain why he kept glancing her way from the stage?

After a few songs, Barrett made his way toward her again. Pretending not to see him, she headed toward the restroom as Laney talked with Meaghan's mother.

The music reverberated within the walls of the restroom, but it was blessedly empty. Grace stared at her reflection in the mirror and took several slow breaths. Being out of sight of Nathan helped her regain some of her sanity. She wasn't the same awestruck girl she'd been in high school, so what she was feeling were just echoes. She wasn't falling into that Nathan Teague trap again.

Footsteps at the entrance to the restroom proved to belong to Laney.

"You okay?" she asked as she approached the sinks and opened her purse.

"Yeah, just tired."

"Yes, I'm sure it must be exhausting dodging all that male attention."

Grace shook her head and unnecessarily

washed her hands. "I think in a previous life you were a pit bull."

Laney laughed. "I did consider law school—for about three seconds. Landed in the exciting world of pharmaceutical sales instead."

"No doubt that's where Cheyenne's go-get-'em attitude comes from."

"Honey, she came out that way." Laney leaned toward the mirror and reapplied her lipstick. "So, are you glad you came tonight?"

"I'm not sure."

Laney capped the coral lipstick and dropped it into her purse, then turned to face Grace. "Old feelings coming back?"

Grace thought about lying but didn't see any reason. Laney would see right through it. "Yeah, but that's all they are—old feelings."

"Tell me, did Nathan look at you like that before?"

"How's that?"

"Like there wasn't another woman around for a hundred miles."

"I can't be sure it's me he wants."

"Oh, trust me, it's you. Even Barrett Farnsley saw it. That's why he's determined to dance with you again. I swear it's a game of testosterone tug-of-war."

Grace glanced toward the doorway. "Is he still out there?"

"Hanging around like a little lovesick puppy."

Grace sighed. "This is so not what I came here for."

"Life has a wicked habit of derailing our best-laid plans."

Grace nodded. "I just came back to make sure Evan would have a home if anything ever happened to me. I knew it'd be hard, but I didn't anticipate all the complications."

"Such as still feeling something for Evan's father."

Two women decked out in crisp new Western attire—tourists, no doubt—came into the restroom, laughing loudly. Grace glanced at Laney, trying to tell her without words that she didn't want to talk about Nathan and Evan with ears around to overhear. Laney nodded. "Want me to run interference with Mr. Puppy Eyes?"

"Would you? I really am tired."

Familiar concern creased Laney's face. "Are you sure you're okay?"

"Yes, stop worrying. Perfectly healthy people get tired, too, you know. I think we'll head back to the ranch and get a good night's rest."

"Okay. Consider the running of interference done."

"Thanks. I owe you."

Laney leaned close. "You can repay me by giving me all the juicy details when you finally give in to your attraction." With a mischievous smile, Laney turned and headed out the door.

Grace waited another minute before leaving the restroom. She spotted Merline and headed her direction, figuring Evan would be within sight of his grandmother. Halfway there, she noticed that Evan was once again sitting on one of the tall stools. But now he had a huge scoop of strawberry ice cream in front of him and a long spoon in his hand.

"Hey, Mom," he said when he spotted her. "Look what Miss Merline got me."

"I see. Did you thank her?"

"He did," Merline said. "He has very good manners."

Evan stuffed another bite of ice cream into his strawberry-rimmed mouth.

"I appreciate you watching him, Merline." A wave of guilt hit her that she was doing all the taking and giving nothing in return. She was asking this kind woman to pretend she didn't know Evan was her grandson.

"Oh, it was fun."

Grace couldn't quite meet the older woman's eyes. Part of her felt selfish and cruel for keeping Evan from Merline. She'd told herself she could keep this trip emotion-free, but she should have known better. She wondered what would happen if she just revealed everything, but then those old fears of having Evan ripped out of her arms came roaring back, shooting a pain so intense through her that it put the cancer to shame.

"Did you like dancing, Mom?"

Grace stiffened at the unexpected question. "Yes, it was nice. Did you?"

Evan scrunched up his face. "The guys were laughing at me."

"You don't pay them any mind," Merline said. "You and Cheyenne were adorable."

Evan looked aghast at the idea, though he did shoot a glance in Cheyenne's direction.

"Did you dance with my daddy like that?" Evan asked.

Grace's heart banged hard against her chest. The kid was killing her.

"Okay, last bite," she said. "We need to get going."

"Already?" Merline asked.

Grace hazarded a glance at Nathan's mother, saw the look of longing in her eyes as she watched Evan take a huge bite of ice cream.

Family means more than anything to my mom.

Those words echoed in Grace's memory,

shaming her. Before she could start hating herself any more than she already did in that moment, she grasped Evan's hand.

"Do we have to go?" he asked.

"Yes, you'll thank me tomorrow. Goodbye, Merline. Thanks again."

She walked slowly enough that Evan could keep up, so it felt like forever before she reached the music hall's exit. Afraid that someone—Merline, Barrett, worst of all, Nathan—would catch her, she resisted the need to pick up Evan and run with him to the car. Her emotions were overloading, like an electric outlet with too many plugs shoved into it. All she needed was some quiet, time to think and sort everything out.

Grace breathed marginally better once they were in the car. Evan had gone quiet in the few short minutes since they'd left Merline, a sure sign he was more tired than he'd ever admit and would likely be asleep well before they reached the ranch.

She turned the keys in the ignition—and nothing happened. The engine didn't even make a feeble attempt to turn over. "You've got to be kidding me."

"What's wrong?" Evan asked in his sleepy voice.

"Nothing, sweetie. The car is just being cranky."

Grace bit her lip and tried again. Maybe if she held her mouth just right. Still nothing. Not even a hint of the dashboard lights illuminating. She caught Evan's eye in the rearview mirror. "Stay here. I need to check something outside."

He nodded slowly.

She popped the hood and slipped out of the car. When she lifted the hood, the blinking neon arrow she'd wished for identifying the problem area wasn't there. The myriad parts that made her car go—normally—sat there silent, mocking her ignorance. A few choice words slipped out.

"Trying to give sailors a run for their money?"

Grace yelped before she realized it wasn't an ax murderer speaking to her. Just the man who'd so upset her equilibrium.

"Sorry, I didn't mean to scare you," Nathan said. "I thought you heard me."

She placed her hands on her hips and stared at the useless hunk of metal that was her car engine. "I guess I was too busy scorching the air."

She half expected him to laugh, but he didn't. "Nothing like a car that won't start to make a person want to cuss. Hang on and I'll give you a jump."

Grace watched him walk away, worried by the distance she now sensed between them. What had happened? Had he decided his wooing tactic wasn't working? Even if he wasn't interested in her, she couldn't let him view her as an adversary. She had to convince him that she truly had Evan's best interests as her utmost priority.

In less than a minute, he pulled his truck next to her car and attached a set of jumper cables to both vehicles.

"Were you all done playing?" she asked.

"Yeah. You cut out early."

She nodded toward the car. "Evan was tired." That's right, she was blaming her hasty departure on her kid. She wasn't about to admit the real reason, that Nathan made her question everything she'd worked out in her mind just by dancing with her, offering her a smile.

"Did he have fun tonight?"

"Yeah. Your mom bought him ice cream. He's had it twice today. I'll be lucky if he doesn't wake up in the middle of the night with a stomachache."

"He'll be fine. I remember sneaking ice

cream or cake in the middle of the night, and it never did me any harm."

A pang of unwanted memory surprised her. "I can't imagine that."

"I had a stomach of steel."

"No, I mean sneaking desserts in the middle of the night. Even having dessert to sneak."

He paused in his movements for a moment before checking the cable connections. "Your mom didn't make desserts?"

"Not often, mainly at Christmas, and then each of us was only allowed one serving." She shrugged. "Of course, when you're feeding that many people, it doesn't last long."

"What about birthdays?"

The image of standing in the grocery store staring at a fancy cake decorated with princesses drifted up from some forgotten recess of her mind. She'd wanted that cake more than she'd ever wanted anything in her life.

"No. They said splurging like that was wasteful."

This time, Nathan cursed. "The more you tell me, the more I want to strangle your parents."

She wasn't a proponent of violence, but something about his words and the way he said them sent warmth flowing through her. In that moment, she wanted to hug him and be hugged by him, but she stood her ground and forced herself to stare at the spot where the jumper cables were affixed to the car's battery. She had to remember that Nathan might be angry at her parents only because their actions led to her keeping Evan from him. No, even if everything he was doing now was to be a part of Evan's life, she didn't believe he was that cold.

After what Nathan decided was the proper amount of time, he told her to try starting the car. She slipped into the driver's seat, noticing that Evan was totally out. When she turned the ignition, nothing happened.

"I'm afraid your battery is shot," he said. "I'll give you a ride back to the ranch, and I'll call Greg over at the garage in the morning to take a look at your car."

The instinct to refuse welled up, but then common sense trumped it. They were going to the same place. Evan was already asleep, and she herself was flagging. Since her illness, she tired more easily and had to get more sleep than she used to. So she nodded. "I'll get Evan."

Nathan disconnected the cables and took care closing the hood as quietly as he could. "I'll get him."

It made sense to let Nathan retrieve Evan.

He might have to take over Evan's care someday, and it was possible it'd be during the years when Nathan might have to secure their son with a seat belt while Evan slept. The thought of dying before Evan grew up broke her heart.

By the time she shook off that morbid thought, Nathan was already leaning into the back of the car. When he emerged with Evan in his arms, her breath caught in her chest. Evan looked so small next to his father, so unaware of who was holding him. But it was the look on Nathan's face that shook her to the deepest part of her soul. He looked at his son as if he were the most precious thing in the world.

Chapter Eight

When they arrived at the ranch, Nathan lifted his son in his arms and carried him toward the cabin. He waited silently as Grace unlocked the door and turned on a lamp.

"That's his room," she said as she pointed toward one of the two bedrooms. They were the first words either of them had spoken since they left town. Nathan wondered if Grace was trying to convince herself it was so they wouldn't wake Evan, the way Nathan was.

The truth? The moment he'd pulled Evan out of Grace's car, his heart swelled with such a surge of love and protectiveness. He couldn't let them leave, not without assurances from

Grace that they'd visit again, that he could visit them. That Evan would know who his father was.

Grace pulled back the cover, and Nathan placed Evan gently in the bed. Grace covered him and soothed him with caresses atop his head when Evan looked as though he might wake up.

"Thank you," she whispered. There was no mistaking her words as anything other than a dismissal.

Nathan managed to clamp a lid down on his anger. Did the woman not think about how it might affect him when he saw her tuck their son into bed the way she'd done hundreds of times? Something he'd never had the opportunity to do because of her decision.

He wanted to argue, but now wasn't the time or place. But there would be a right time and place. He retreated but stopped at the bedroom door to take one more look at Evan, his son. The enormity of that relationship threatened to fell him. He felt like a different man when he thought of himself as a father. He knew, in his bones, he'd be a good one—if Grace would only let him.

Or if he took matters into his own hands.

He left the two of them alone and headed

outside, but he didn't leave. He crossed the space between Grace's cabin and a gap in the trees that afforded a view of the main part of the ranch. This late, all he saw were the lights burning in his parents' living room, near the corrals and over the entrance to the barn.

He parked himself atop a picnic table next to the cabin's outdoor grill so he could think about what to do next. He could fight her for Evan, but that didn't feel right. Plus, she'd evidently taken very good care of Evan and the boy loved his mother. Nathan wasn't going to be the bad guy here, but he wasn't going to just roll over, either. He still felt winning Grace over was the best plan, but he wasn't ruling out legal options if it came to that.

Enough time passed that he wondered if Grace had gone to bed, as well. Or maybe she was simply avoiding him. But no sooner had that thought formed than he heard the front door open then close with a soft click. He didn't speak as she approached, didn't voice his suspicions.

"I think he's out for the night," Grace said as she came closer. "I haven't seen him sleep that deeply in a long time."

Don't be confrontational. Play it cool.

"Long day of cowboying and dancing will do that to a guy."

She didn't turn toward him, but he detected her smile as she pulled herself up on the table. Not too close, but near enough that it brought back all the attraction he'd felt toward her earlier in the evening. An attraction that made the entire situation all the more confusing. If it weren't for the little fact she'd hidden his son from him, he thought he might welcome her back into his life, see where this attraction went. Was that possible?

"I'd forgotten how quiet it can be out here," she said.

"Yeah, still a few places in the world where you can hear your thoughts."

She glanced toward him. "Not a fan of cities, huh?"

"They're nice enough to visit." When she didn't say anything, he asked, "Do you like it?"

She nodded. "I have friends there, my business."

"How did you get into that?"

"Interior design?"

"Yeah." Despite everything, he found her easy to talk to. Now that he thought about it, she'd been that way in high school, too, even if she'd been shy then.

She seemed to think for a minute, maybe searching for the moment she'd made the decision. "I went into college undeclared, just glad to be there. I didn't know what I wanted to be, hadn't even allowed myself to think about the future beyond taking care of Evan in a long time." She shook her head slowly. "I didn't even really know who I was. It was actually my friend Emily, who's my business partner now, who suggested interior design. I had this knack for decorating our dump of an apartment on next to nothing."

"Design on a Dime?"

She shot him a look of surprise.

He shrugged. "Mom watches a lot of HGTV."

Grace laughed. "Sure."

"She does."

Grace's smile took his breath away.

"I know. She told me that on the first day."

"So you just like to tease me?"

"It has its moments." She shifted her attention to the slice of moon visible through the tops of the pines. "I always liked pretty things—clothes, furnishings, didn't matter—but my parents were adamant that it was sinful to want anything that wasn't a necessity to live. I guess somewhere along the way some part of me decided I wanted to make the world beautiful for other people."

Before he thought about it, Nathan reached over and took her hand. He told himself that it was just part of his plan to gain her trust, so why did touching her feel so good? Grace surprised him by not pulling away.

"I'm glad you have those pretty things in your life now." He found truth in those words. She'd had enough of the ugly side of life at the hands of her parents.

She returned the gentle pressure where their hands touched. "Thank you."

Several moments passed in which the only sounds were a gentle breeze whistling through the pines and a motor going up the drive to the main house, his parents coming home from the music hall.

Suddenly, Grace pointed toward the sky. "Did you see that?"

He looked up but only saw the moon and a sprinkling of stars. "What?"

"A shooting star," she said with undisguised wonder in her voice. He doubted she even realized it. How often had she seen them as a child and wished for a different life?

"Guess you better make a wish."

"If only it were that simple."

"Can't hurt." He looked up at the sky again. "What would you wish for?"

A couple of seconds ticked by, enough time that it seemed Grace had considered more than one answer before speaking. "That Evan would have a long and healthy life."

It sounded like the wish of a loving mother, an appropriate wish, but something about it seemed off and he couldn't figure out why.

Grace pulled her hand away from his and slid off the table. "I think the day is catching up with me, too. I need to hit the hay."

He walked with her back to the front of the cabin, but when she turned for the front steps he reached out and grasped her hand again. An unfamiliar, jittery feeling accompanied the thought that he didn't want the night to end.

"I had a nice time tonight," he said when her gaze met his.

Her lips curved into a small smile. Nothing too committal but not too closed off, either. "I did, too."

The silence stretched between them. He knew she would pull away again, and the image of her dancing with Barrett Farnsley, of them laughing together, slammed into him. A crazy, wild, out-of-nowhere desperation seized him. What was going on?

"Well, I better go—"

Nathan closed the distance between them and turned her face up. He registered her wide eyes a moment before he kissed her.

Nathan's lips against hers catapulted Grace back in time, to that night when he'd been the first boy to ever kiss her. The first one to make her heart beat so impossibly fast. As it was doing now. Some remnant of sanity told her to pull away, but she didn't. She wanted this, had wanted it since the first moment she'd set eyes on him again. It'd been so long since she'd allowed herself to want something this much, just for herself.

So she kissed him back with all the feeling she'd been too young and inexperienced to show him before. He tasted of coffee and something sweet. His arms went around her, pulling her closer. He deepened the kiss, drugging her mind and body with a combustible desire.

She feared she could have stayed there kissing him all night if it wasn't for the sound of a car engine approaching. Grace stepped quickly away, but she couldn't look at him. What had she done? Now he knew just how he affected her, and that gave him too much power.

"Good night, Nathan." She hurried into the cabin just as headlights illuminated the porch. Even the shut and locked door behind her back didn't make her feel safe. She stood leaning against the door, her heart beating so fast and hard she could barely hear above the rushing of her pulse. Her skin flushed at the memory of his hands on her, his lips dueling with her own.

Grace lifted her fingertips to her lips, relived those delicious kisses once again. Then she closed her eyes and leaned her head back against the door.

What had she done?

She couldn't face him.

That was the first thought Grace had when she awoke the next morning after pitifully little sleep. And she had the perfect excuse. Two, actually.

When she heard Laney and Cheyenne come outside next door, she hurried Evan onto the porch.

"Laney?"

Her friend turned and waved. Grace urged Evan forward, but he was dragging his feet. She suspected it had something to do with the big smile Cheyenne was aiming toward him. He seemed to be in the same conflicted-feelings boat about Cheyenne as Grace was about Nathan.

"I thought you were already gone," Laney said when they drew near.

"My car wouldn't start last night. It's going into the shop this morning."

"So Nathan gave you a ride back?"

Grace stopped in her tracks and met Laney's all-too-knowing gaze.

"I saw him leaving as we pulled in."

"Uh, yeah, I didn't want to pull you all away from the dance early, and he was nice enough to give us a lift."

"Hmm." There was a lot of meaning in that *hmm* that thankfully went over the kids' heads.

"I was wondering if Evan could ride down with you. I've actually got to get some work done today, especially since I'm evidently going to have unexpected car repairs."

"Sure."

"Thanks."

"Okay, go on, you two," Laney said. "In the back you go."

As the kids climbed into opposite sides of the SUV, Laney sidled up next to Grace. "I do feel like I'm missing some juicy details." She made a teasing, tutting sound. "However will we cure that?"

"I'm convinced you and Emily were separated at birth." With that, Grace turned and headed back toward the cabin, the sound of Laney's laughter following her.

Grace tried to work, really she did. After a check-in call with Emily, she parked herself at the desk next to the window and sketched some ideas for an attorney's second home in the Ozarks. By the time she'd wadded up and discarded half a dozen failed attempts, she closed her sketchbook and walked to the kitchen to get a drink of water. She downed an entire glass as she watched a black-and-yellow oriole survey his surroundings from his perch atop the picnic table.

She paced across the cabin, considered walking down to the main part of the ranch to see what Nathan had the kids doing today. At some point, she'd known each day's schedule, but her brain had ceased to function properly the moment Nathan had kissed her last night.

What had she been thinking, kissing him? She'd asked herself that same question at least a dozen times but had yet to come up with an answer that didn't involve her taking a complete and utter leave of her senses.

The warmth and rush of desire she'd experienced the night before sluiced through her again. She had to get out of the cabin, do something to rid herself of the anxious energy that wouldn't let her concentrate on anything but replaying those kisses over and over until she was on the verge of hunting down Nathan and dragging him off to the nearest private spot.

She headed out the door, not even sure where she was going. The ranch had several walking trails, and she remembered passing the trailhead for one on her way up to the cabins. The trail wound through stands of live oaks, their curling limbs as intriguing as they'd ever been when she'd been a girl. She used to daydream about building her own little house high up in the tallest live oak she could find, up where no one would ever find her.

The higher the trail climbed, the better she felt. With each step, the tension eased and she breathed more deeply of the fresh Hill Country air. This part of Texas really was a beautiful place, if only there weren't so many bad memories attached to it. The trees began to grow fewer in number. She should probably turn back, but she couldn't force herself to do it, couldn't stand the idea of sitting in that claustrophobic cabin or, worse, facing Nathan without any idea how she was going to react.

She had to let him know that what had

happened between them didn't change anything. The life she'd built for Evan and herself was still back in Arkansas. She'd worked too hard to throw all that accomplishment, all that safety away just because Nathan Teague could still make her pulse race.

Grace rounded a curve in the trail and found herself on the edge of a meadow filled to bursting with bluebonnets. She gasped at the unparalleled beauty, like a great blue sea, and carefully walked forward.

"Beautiful, isn't it?"

Grace jumped at the out-of-place sound of another person's voice. She spun and found herself staring at Merline, who sat higher up at the back edge of the meadow. She appeared to be facing a canvas and held a paintbrush in her hand. A wide, straw hat shaded her face from the bright sun.

"It is." Grace let her gaze wander over the blue-tinged meadow again. "I don't think I've ever seen a more beautiful spot."

"It's my favorite part of the ranch. Hank brought me here when we were dating, about this time of year. I knew I either had to marry him or convince him to sell me the ranch." Merline chuckled at the memory. "I'm surprised to see you up here though. You don't leave Evan's side much."

Grace shifted, uncomfortable talking to Merline about Evan when there was no one else around as a buffer, afraid the older woman might finally tell her exactly what she thought of Grace and her decision to keep Evan away from not only Nathan but the rest of the Teagues, as well. The ones who'd done her no harm.

The guilt ate at her until it burst out in the form of an apology. "I'm sorry."

"For what, dear?" Why did Merline have to be so nice? It made everything harder.

"For…" She choked, finding it difficult to push the words she needed to say past the growing lump in her throat. "For not telling you all about Evan."

Merline didn't immediately respond, seeming to take a few moments to collect her thoughts. Maybe she was as surprised to hear the apology as Grace was at offering it.

"I won't lie and say I wasn't upset when I found out. We all were. This may come as a surprise to you, but part of me understands, too."

"How could you?"

"I always figure people have reasons for doing what they do, and I try to put myself in their shoes to see what things look like from that perspective."

Grace looked at the other woman, liking her even more and feeling worse about keeping her grandson from her. "That's a rare quality."

"I'll take that as a compliment."

"It was."

Merline redirected her gaze out across the field of wildflowers. "Sometimes we do things we think are right at the time that may prove not to be later. But none of us can see the future, so we just do the best we can."

"I never meant to hurt anyone. It's just that…" Grace swallowed against that damn lump again, feeling as if she was losing her grasp on the control she so desperately needed.

"You don't have to explain. That's for you and Nathan to discuss. But I knew your parents. They are hard people, and they've done you wrong more than once. That said, I hope you can get past the fear they caused you. We all want Evan in our lives. You, too."

Tears pooled in Grace's eyes and she had to look away. She focused on a single bluebonnet, trying to keep the tears from breaking free.

"Well, I suspect you went for a walk to have some alone time. This is a good place to sort out thoughts. I've done that myself many times. I'll go and give you some privacy." Merline stood and started assembling her supplies.

Even though the thought of sitting in this spot of ultimate peace alone was exactly what Grace wanted, she didn't feel right about interrupting Merline. Especially when the other woman had a lot on her mind, too. "No, you were here first." Desperate for something else to say, anything not related to Evan, she nodded toward the canvas. "I didn't know you painted."

"I dabble. Used to paint more when I was young. Then I got busy raising boys and working. You know how it is. I picked it back up a couple of years ago when I was cleaning out the attic and found some of my old paints."

"Mind if I see?"

"Of course not. Don't expect Monet or O'Keefe though."

Grace approached the canvas, but she wasn't prepared for the image that greeted her. The shades of blue in the painting were every bit as vibrant and lifelike as their real-life models.

"Merline, this is gorgeous."

"Aw, that's a nice thing to say."

"No, I'm not just saying it. It's wonderful, exhibit quality. Have you ever shown your work at a gallery?"

Merline waved away the idea. "Heavens, no. I've never shown them to anyone."

"You're kidding me."

Merline shook her head. "Not even Hank."

"Well, then that's a crime. You really ought to show this off. I bet the shops in town would go crazy for them."

"Now I'm sure you're overstating things."

Grace took Merline's hand and pulled the older woman to her side. She pointed toward the drying painting. "Look at that and tell me it doesn't take your breath away."

Merline stared at her work, her "dabbling." "You really think it's good?"

"Yes. I buy art for clients all the time. I know what I'm talking about. You should have your own gallery when you get enough pieces."

Merline laughed. "Honey, I have an attic full of paintings. Would you like to see them?"

Grace hesitated, not wanting to venture so close to Nathan yet, but her eye for beautiful things and her curiosity demanded she see more.

"If you don't mind me traipsing through your attic."

Luck was smiling at her this morning. When they reached Merline and Hank's house, Nathan was occupied inside the barn with the kids. She followed Merline past the dining room table where Grace had helped Nathan grasp enough algebra to scrape by with a C. They took a set of stairs she'd never seen at the back of the house that led to not exactly an attic but to a small, finished bonus room. Merline hadn't been lying. Canvases of various sizes leaned against every wall.

Grace tilted back the one nearest her and saw the vibrant red of Indian paintbrush in the foreground and a giant live oak tree in the background. A tiny canvas revealed a single pink primrose, its delicate petals so real Grace thought for a moment she could see it wave in an evening breeze. Each canvas revealed another slice of the Hill Country in all its colorful beauty. There were adequate paintings of barns and cowboys, but it was the wildflowers that were filled with soul.

"You like the wildflowers the best, don't you?" Grace asked.

"Yes. It shows?"

Grace nodded then met Merline's gaze. "This is amazing. You shouldn't hide talent like this."

Merline looked around the room as if she was seeing it for the first time. "I was just doing it for fun, to relax. I never thought beyond that."

"Well, I am."

"You really think they're gallery quality?" Merline scanned the room with a look of disbelief.

"I do."

Grace's phone rang in her pocket. "Excuse me." She walked to the edge of the room and answered while watching Merline run her fingertips softly over a painting of some type of yellow wildflowers lining a dirt road. "Hello?"

"Ms. Cameron, we've got your car ready."

A few seconds of conversation revealed she'd had a dead battery and corroded battery cables, but the car was running great now. Grace thanked the mechanic and said she'd pick it up as soon as she could. As she hung up, she was already planning to ask Laney to take her into town. Riding with Nathan again was way too dangerous now. She somehow had to get through the rest of the week so she could put several hundred miles between them. A buffer against her own weakness.

"I take it your car is ready," Merline said as she shifted her attention from her expanse of paintings back to Grace.

"Yeah. I'll have Laney take me to pick it up later."

"No need. I can take you now."

"Oh, I don't want to inconvenience you." And despite their friendly conversation, she wasn't sure she was ready to be trapped alone in a car with a wronged grandmother.

Merline waved a hand. "I have to go to the grocery anyway. All these men around here are bottomless pits."

Grace laughed, surprised by how easily Merline could put her at ease. "They must start that early. I'm surprised Evan isn't twice his size."

Merline smiled. "He's an energetic boy, still able to burn off all those calories almost as soon as he eats them."

It should have felt awkward talking to Merline about her grandson when Grace still hadn't revealed that relationship to Evan. But it wasn't. It felt oddly natural. When she thought back, it made sense. On the days when Grace had come to the ranch for tutoring sessions with Nathan, Merline had made her feel welcome, more than welcome. She distinctly remembered wishing her own mother were more like Merline. Grace fought against a truth rising in her—that she should share Evan with his father's family.

She swallowed past the lump forming in her throat. The Teagues had done nothing to indicate they would try to take Evan from her, so why couldn't she just do as Merline suggested—let go of that fear and see where revelation led?

Because the last time she'd loosened her grip on him, he had been stolen from her. And while her mind knew her family and the Teagues were nothing alike, that dark, curling fear residing close to her heart whispered that if she let go, even the merest bit, she'd lose her son again. And this time, she might not get him back.

Merline moved toward the stairs. "Just let me grab my list and we'll head into town."

Grace followed her through the kitchen and out the back to where Merline's small SUV was parked. She glanced toward the barn.

"Don't worry about Evan," Merline said. "Nathan and the rest of the guys will take care of him until you get back."

Grace still hesitated, an irrational fear attacking her.

Merline was quiet for several seconds before speaking again. "Nathan won't do anything until you give him permission."

Grace gave Merline the briefest glance before lowering her gaze to the ground. Nathan hadn't asked for permission to kiss her the night before. He'd just taken what he wanted. Would he do the same with his son?

Chapter Nine

"You're going to spoil that horse rotten," Nathan said as he walked up next to Evan.

His son froze in the process of feeding a carrot stick to Dolly. "I'm sorry."

Nathan reached over and squeezed Evan's shoulder. "It's okay. I'm just teasing you."

Evan hesitated, as if he thought Nathan might be lying to him, before giving the carrot to Dolly. The boy rubbed Dolly's nose and laughed when she snorted.

"Looks like you two have become good friends." Nathan leaned his arms on the top of the fence.

"Yeah. I like her."

Nathan glanced back over his shoulder to where the rest of the campers and their parents were eating lunch on the picnic tables behind the house. Little Cheyenne was watching Evan's every move. "I don't think Dolly is the only girl who likes you."

Evan looked up at him with the cluelessness of a six-year-old boy. Nathan nodded over his shoulder. Evan's expression changed and he didn't look behind him.

Nathan had to laugh. "Not interested in girls yet?"

"Eww, no." Funny how the boy said one thing but still glanced toward the picnic area.

Nathan laughed again, trying to remember if he'd felt that way about girls at the same age—interested but not willing to admit it. But the image that came to mind was of Grace when he'd kissed her the night before. The softness of her lips, the curves of her body so close to his own had fueled an unexpected burst of desire in him. If Cheyenne's mom hadn't picked that inopportune moment to return to her cabin, he wondered where those kisses would have led.

Most likely, Grace would have still pulled away. Her fear and caution would have probably won out over whatever attraction she was feeling for him. But just the possibility that the kisses might have led elsewhere, perhaps to Grace's bed, had kept him awake a good long while after he'd returned to his cabin on the other side of the ranch. When he'd fallen asleep, he'd dreamed of her, a series of images of the younger Grace mixed with the present-day Grace. When he'd woken that morning just as dream Grace was naked and eager beneath him, he'd found himself in an uncomfortable state and cursed.

And he shouldn't be thinking about that sort of thing while standing next to his son.

"Do you have any animals at home?" Nathan asked as he scratched Dolly between her ears.

"A dog. His name is Frosty."

"I'm guessing he's white."

"Yeah. Big and fluffy. Mom says I used to try to ride him when I was little, but I don't remember that."

When he was little. He was still little to Nathan, a miniature version of himself and Grace.

Evan let out a sigh. "I would love to have a horse."

It was on the tip of Nathan's tongue to tell him he could have one now, that Nathan would go riding with him every day. But he couldn't do that, not yet. He had to give convincing Grace it was okay to reveal the truth a chance. "Maybe someday."

Evan just sighed again, as if he thought the possibility as remote as traveling to the North Pole to meet Santa Claus.

"Until then, you can look forward to the trail ride in a couple of days."

"Can I ride Dolly?"

"If you want to."

"Awesome!"

Nathan chuckled at Evan's enthusiastic response and resisted the urge to ruffle his hair. Instead, he turned around and faced the barn. "So, which horse do you think your mom would like to ride?"

Evan shrugged. "I don't know if she can ride a horse. We ride bikes all the time, but not horses."

The image of the two of them riding bikes side by side left Nathan with a yawning sense of loss. He should have been there, too, seeing his son's milestones like first steps and first bike ride without training wheels. He hated the thought of all the things he would miss if he couldn't convince Grace to change her mind. Things like the day when the admiration of a pretty girl wouldn't elicit an "eww" from Evan.

He needed to explore what other options were open to him if she refused to budge. He shifted from one foot to the other, uncomfortable with the idea of going behind her back, of doing something that might hurt her all over again. She'd been through enough. But did all she'd endured give her the right to keep his son from him? No.

"Let's visit the horses, and maybe you can pick out one for your mom."

Evan nodded and shoved his fingers in his back pockets as he headed toward the barn. Nathan couldn't move for a moment. That gesture—had Evan picked it up from him since being on the ranch, or was it just further evidence that Evan was a lot like him?

He caught sight of Cheyenne's mom watching him. It wasn't the appreciative glances women often tossed his way, but rather one of knowing. He got the distinct impression that she knew exactly how he and Evan were related. He'd seen Grace and her spending a lot of time together. Had Grace told her the truth? Or was it as obvious as his family said?

Nathan broke eye contact and followed Evan into the barn. They made their way past each stall, debating the pros and cons of each horse.

"How about this one?" Nathan caressed the forehead of Hazel, a dappled gray mare.

Evan's forehead scrunched. "She's awfully big. I don't want Mom to fall off and get hurt."

It wasn't the first time Evan had said something that gave Nathan the impression he was protective of Grace. He wondered where that came from. Was it because he considered himself the "man" of the family? Surely she hadn't told him about what her parents had done.

"Hazel is a good, calm horse. And she won't look as big to your mom as she does to you."

Evan chewed his bottom lip as he stared at the horse.

"I'll make sure your mom is safe, just like I will for you." Something warm and tender moved in Nathan's heart when he realized the absolute, deep truth of those words. Despite that knot of betrayal that still reared its head, he wanted to keep them both safe, from everything. But how could he do that if they were an entire state away?

Evan nodded. "Okay."

"Now that we have that settled, I think I know some chocolate chip cookies that are calling my name."

"Mine, too!"

As they turned to leave the barn, Evan surprised Nathan by grabbing his hand. For a moment, his heart forgot to beat correctly. But then it settled, accepting the gesture as right and good. When they emerged from the shade of the barn into the bright sunlight, Nathan's heart had never felt so full.

As they rolled into Blue Falls, Grace tried to imagine what it would have been like to finish growing up here, if she and Nathan hadn't had sex at that party. Would she have broken free of her parents, or would they have managed to break her down to the point where she followed in their footsteps? A chill ran the length of her spine at the thought of turning out like them. Cold and unyielding. From where she sat now, she couldn't imagine it. She liked to think she'd have had the strength and nerve to walk away and live the life she'd always wanted.

But she wouldn't have Evan. Despite everything, she'd go through it all again to have her son.

"You okay?" Merline asked.

Grace glanced over at the other woman. "Yeah. Just thinking how it seems like forever since I've been here and feels like yesterday at the same time."

Merline nodded. "Funny how time messes with our minds like that. I still look at my boys and wonder how in the world they got to be grown men and I turned into an old, wrinkly woman."

"You are not old and wrinkly. In fact, you know who I think you look like?"

"I hate to even imagine."

"Helen Mirren."

"Oh, now you're just being silly. That woman is gorgeous. I wasn't that pretty when I was twenty, let alone now."

"Hmm, I think maybe you're looking at yourself with the same eyes you used to look at your artwork."

Merline reached across the console and squeezed Grace's hand. "You are the sweetest girl. My son has good taste."

Grace couldn't have been more shocked by the other woman's words. Surely she hadn't heard Merline right. Some weak, lonely part of her mind must have manufactured those words and layered them over whatever Merline had really said. Grace pulled her hand from Merline's grasp.

"It's obvious he still has feelings for you," Merline said.

"I'm sorry, but you're mistaken. There were never any feelings to still have."

"I think you're wrong."

Grace took a deep breath. "The fact that Nathan is Evan's father is the result of a single incident. I won't call it a mistake because I love Evan more than life itself, but it wasn't anything romantic or lasting." At least not on Nathan's part.

Then why had he kissed her? Part of her wanted to believe it had nothing to do with Evan, but letting herself want that left her too open to being hurt by him again.

"I don't know what happened, and now that you're both adults it's not really any of my business. All I ask is that you give Nathan a chance."

Grace didn't know if Merline meant a chance to be with Evan or her, but it didn't matter. Both had their own set of dangers. And Merline had a vested interest in seeing Grace stay in Blue Falls.

Merline made a right turn off Main Street onto Lakeview. They passed small businesses and homes with second-story balconies built to enjoy the beautiful view of the lake and falls. As they rounded a corner, she spotted a vacant building with a big picture window and beautiful landscaping filled with rocks and native plants. A "For Sale" sign stood at an angle at the edge of the rock garden.

"Stop!"

Merline hit the brakes. "What's wrong?"

Grace pointed toward a small parking area beside the building. "Pull in here."

Merline did as she asked without questioning why. When Merline parked, Grace hopped out and walked toward the front of the building. She approached the picture window and pressed her face to the glass to look inside. Just as she'd thought—the space inside was open with a counter in one of the front corners. The vaulted ceilings gave the space a soaring feel.

"Why did you want to stop?" Merline asked when she caught up to her.

Grace stepped back from the window and pointed toward the interior of the building. "This is the perfect spot for your art gallery."

"What?"

"The space is perfect, with some adjustments of course."

"I don't know."

The familiar excitement that came with new design projects nearly had Grace hopping. "Let's call the real estate agent, get a look inside."

"I've been inside, when it was a clothing store a year or so ago."

"But you weren't thinking in art gallery terms at that point." Before Merline could nix the idea, Grace pulled out her cell phone and called the number on the "For Sale" sign. The agent said she could be there in five minutes.

During their wait, Grace tried to drum up equal excitement in Merline by leading her around the outside of the property. She pointed toward the back corner. "You could put some benches and a sundial there. And maybe enlist other artists to display some outdoor art pieces along the fence."

"Sounds like you've already got some great plans," said a thirtyish woman with hip-length blond hair as she approached. "I'm Justine Ware. Nice to meet you." She extended her hand for Grace to shake.

"Grace Cameron. Thanks for coming over so quickly."

"You caught me at a good time." Justine shifted her attention to her left. "Merline, didn't expect to see you here."

"I didn't expect to be here."

Confusion made its way into Justine's expression.

"It was my idea to stop," Grace said. "Can we take a look inside?"

"Sure. I think you'll really like the space. Very open and inviting. What are you thinking of putting in?"

"An art gallery."

"Oh, that sounds great. Some changes in the lighting fixtures, maybe the addition of a couple of display walls in the middle of the space would really make it work."

As they stepped inside and Grace got a closer look at the interior, she agreed with Justine. Already she was picturing Merline's paintings on white walls and some plain display pedestals for other artists' three-dimensional art pieces. Furnishings and accents in various blues to capture the feel of the lake and the profusion of bluebonnets around it.

When Justine excused herself to take a call, Grace turned to Merline. "What do you think? I know the asking price is a bit steep, but with the current market I bet you could get the owner to come down significantly."

"I'm less worried about that than I am that I'm even contemplating this. I feel like I've misplaced my common sense."

"You haven't. Trust me, life is too short to not go after things that will bring joy to your life and those of others."

When Merline gave her a questioning look, Grace realized she'd maybe revealed too much. To cover up her slip, she started walking around the room, telling Merline some of her ideas to help dispel the last of Merline's hesitance. After she finished, Merline stood in the middle of the room, a smile on her face. Grace had won her over, given her a glimpse of what this place could be.

"I'll have to talk to Hank, but I'm leaning toward doing it."

"You won't be sorry."

"I just have one condition."

"What's that?"

Merline met Grace's gaze. "That you help me with the design."

"I'm happy to outline some ideas, but you'll have to hire someone local to implement them. We go home this weekend."

A suspended moment passed before Merline nodded, though it was obvious the gesture was forced. But as Grace watched the other woman, she got the distinct impression that she had something up her proverbial sleeve.

Nathan hadn't seen Grace all day, and that bugged him way more than it should. While he was enjoying spending extra time with Evan, he kept looking up to see if she'd made an appearance. After his dad told him that his mom had taken Grace to town to retrieve her car, his heart leapt a little with each sound of an approaching vehicle.

"It's your turn," Evan said.

Nathan shifted his attention back to his son and all the other faces turned his way. After the day's activities with the horses were over and the rest of the guests had headed back to their cabins to prepare for whatever they had planned for the evening, Nathan's father had suggested a game of horseshoes. Nathan and Evan versus Hank and Ryan. Simon, who was off duty, served as the judge. Evan, who was beyond excited to get extra time with anything having to do with cowboys and horses, had been all for it.

Nathan stepped forward and aimed his horseshoe at the opposite stake. When he let it fly, it came within a couple of inches of its destination. He stepped aside so that Evan could take his place. He watched as Evan eyed the stake, made sure he was holding the horseshoe the way Nathan had showed him, bit his bottom lip and threw.

The feet separating the two sand pits was a long distance for such a little guy to cover, but he actually did pretty well. That, combined with his uncle and grandfather deliberately throwing less accurately than Nathan knew they could, had Evan and him comfortably in the lead.

"Looks like Evan is giving you a run for your money, Pops," Simon said with a laugh.

He leaned down toward Evan and spoke in a conspiratorial whisper. “He’s always beating us at horseshoes and rubbing it in. Don’t tell him, but I’m rooting for you to win.”

Evan smiled wide and walked as if he was twice his height toward the opposite pit.

In that moment, Nathan imagined a dozen things he could do with his son. Horseback riding, watching a rodeo while eating corndogs, teaching him to fish. His mom could share all the family photos and tell him the Teague family history. His father could take him for long drives around the ranch, telling his grandson how the ranch had been in the family for generations. Ryan might even give him lessons in woodworking. And Simon? Well, Nathan guessed his older brother could keep his nephew out of trouble by telling him about what happens to people who break the law.

But any of those things happening depended on Grace. And the fact that she seemed to be avoiding him today wasn’t a good sign that she might relent and let him be a part of Evan’s life.

The sound of a vehicle approaching drew his attention again, but Nathan deliberately didn’t look toward it. After a few seconds, the vehicle proved to be his mother’s anyway. When she stepped out of the truck, he noticed Grace wasn't with her. He knew she wouldn't be, so why the inexplicable letdown?

"Don't just stand there, you lot," his mom said when she spotted them. "Help me carry these groceries in."

As one, they all moved away from the horseshoe pit toward the SUV. They each grabbed a couple of bags. Even Evan was tasked with carrying in a ten-pound bag of potatoes.

"Thank you, young man," his mom said when they stepped into the kitchen and Evan handed her the potatoes.

"Hey, we've been carrying in groceries for years, and this one gets the thanks." Simon bent down and attempted to tickle Evan.

Evan laughed and ran around to the other side of the kitchen's island. Thankfully, he was too young to realize he was being singled out from the rest of the campers and why. And Nathan was sure Grace wouldn't like it. But despite knowing that, he made no move to stop it. Maybe if she saw how well Evan fit in here, she'd let go of some of her fear and allow Evan to have more family than just her and some maternal relatives Nathan was certain she would never let their son meet.

"Do you like spaghetti?" his mom asked Evan.

"Yeah. Aunt Emily makes really good spaghetti."

"Oh?"

His mom made eye contact with him. "Grace's business partner."

She nodded. "I have a secret recipe for my spaghetti sauce. Would you like to try it?"

Nathan saw where this conversation was going—a family night even though it wasn't Thursday. He hoped Grace would forgive him for not halting it. He didn't need to hand her any more reasons to be wary of him.

"Sure, if Mom says it's okay." He looked toward the back door, a worried look on his face. "Where is Mom?"

There it was again, that protectiveness toward his mother. Maybe Evan was just naturally protective. After all, his mother was probably everything to him, his link to security and love.

"She should be back soon. I dropped her off to get your car."

"Oh."

"She's probably too tired to go out tonight though," Nathan's mom said. "I think the two of you should have dinner with us. Spaghetti, garlic bread, salad, a big strawberry cake. And you know what else?"

Evan shook his head.

"We're going to play charades afterward."

Everyone in the room other than Nathan's mom and Evan groaned. Evan laughed. "Good. Mom is terrible at charades."

After a pause, everyone broke out into laughter.

Chapter Ten

All the way back to the ranch, Grace wondered what on earth had possessed her to get even more involved with the Teague family. Wasn't she here in Blue Falls just to make in-case arrangements for Evan, nothing more? She hadn't planned on working with Merline to design an art gallery. Hadn't planned on still being so drawn to Nathan. Really hadn't planned on kissing him.

As she made the turn into the ranch, she reminded herself that soon she and Evan would be back home and things could get back to normal. She'd let him enjoy the rest of his cowboy camp, and she could avoid Nathan by working in town at the gallery building. She knew she was taking a risk letting Evan spend so much time with the Teagues without her around, but the thought of facing Nathan again had all of her nerves firing and her palms sweating. If she was honest with herself, she was afraid that come the end of the week, she might be the one who didn't want to leave.

When she pulled into the parking spot closest to the barn, her heart sped up. From the lack of vehicles and the emptiness of the corral, she guessed the day's activities were finished. So where was Evan?

She hurried out of the car and looked inside the barn. Nobody but horses there. Then she heard a burst of laughter from Merline and Hank's house. Evan had to be there, safe. She barely kept herself from running toward the screened back door. When she heard Evan's voice, she stopped and forced her breathing to slow before approaching the door.

"Sounds like something's funny in here," she said as lightheartedly as she could.

"Yes, your son was just telling us how abysmal you are at charades," Simon said.

Merline swatted her oldest son and waved at Grace. "Come on in. We didn't hear you pull up. Of course, it's difficult to hear an explosion over this bunch."

Grace would really rather Evan just come outside so they could return to the relative safety of their cabin, but to say so would be rude. But if she was going to spend time with Merline over the next couple of days, and she didn't want to risk the possibility of the Teagues giving her any trouble over Evan, she had to tread carefully.

She opened the door and stepped inside. Though she was intensely aware of Nathan standing near the wall to her left, she refused to make eye contact with him. Could he feel the heat radiating off her as if she was a walking, talking furnace?

"So how in the world did my lack of skill at charades come up?" she asked as she gently pulled Evan to her side.

"We're playing tonight after dinner," Merline said.

Evan looked up at Grace. "Miss Merline says she makes a special spaghetti sauce. Do you think it's as good as Aunt Emily's?"

"I'm sure it's very good, sweetie."

"And we're having strawberry cake, too, made with real strawberries."

We? Suddenly lightheaded, Grace gripped the edge of the island's marble top.

"Are you okay?" This from Hank, who said so little that it was always a surprise when he did speak.

Grace nodded. "Yeah. Just a little tired." She had to think of a graceful way to get out of this dinner. This *family* dinner.

"Did you eat any lunch?" Merline asked.

Grace thought back over the day. Between the walk up to the field of bluebonnets and the trip to town, she'd somehow forgotten to eat. "I snacked." If you counted the microwave popcorn she'd had while trying to work that morning.

"You go have a seat until dinner," Merline said.

"No, it's okay," Grace said with a layer of meaning that was lost on no one but Evan. "We don't want to impose."

"You're not imposing. After all, we've got a lot to talk about."

Grace's heart skipped a beat until she realized Merline was most likely referring to the gallery and not the fact that Evan was the littlest Teague in the room. At least she hoped so.

"Why do I have the feeling the womenfolk have got something besides dinner cooking?" Hank said.

"Because you're a smart man." Merline

smiled at her husband, a smile that spoke of years of shared love between them. Grace wondered what that kind of love would be like. Would she ever know? Would she manage to open herself up long enough to experience it if it happened her way?

Despite her desire to leave, Grace found herself sliding onto one of the kitchen stools. The lack of food and the constant worry that somebody was going to let the truth slip in front of Evan left her legs weak and threatening to buckle beneath her. Nathan moved in her periphery, but still she kept her eyes away from him.

She listened as Merline related how they'd met up in the field that morning, how she'd shown Grace her dozens of paintings, and how by the end of the day they'd started planning a gallery.

"I thought about it some more on the way home, and I really like the idea of it featuring the artwork of other local artists, too," Merline said. "Your furniture, too, Ryan. That way I won't feel so weird about it being just me on display."

"Why haven't we ever seen these paintings?" Ryan asked. He, too, was a man of few words, so like his father.

Merline shrugged as she stirred the pot of spaghetti just beginning to boil. "I never thought of them as anything more than a hobby."

"Seems I remember saying the same thing about my furniture until someone convinced me otherwise."

"He's got you there, Mom," Simon said, then popped some mixed nuts from a bowl on the island into his mouth.

Hank shifted his attention to Grace. "And you think the gallery is the way to go?"

"I do. I mean, she could put them in some of the other shops in town, but this way she'd be in control of their display, retain more of the profits. Honestly, they deserve more space than any of the other shops would be able to give her."

"That good, huh?"

Grace managed a smile at the dawning pride on Hank's face. "Some of the best I've ever seen."

While Merline continued to work on dinner, the family gathered around the island and brainstormed what seemed like every aspect of the gallery. The more they talked about it, the more everyone got excited. It was impossible not to be infected with the same excitement.

This was the creative process that fueled the aspects of Grace's life that didn't involve Evan. Still, by the time they finished large slices of Merline's to-die-for strawberry cake, Grace was about to pass out from fatigue.

"I hate to be a party pooper, but I'm fading fast," she said.

She thought Evan might object, but when she glanced at him, he was wearing a familiar expression of worry. One she'd hoped never to see again. She offered him a big smile to help reassure him.

"I think you're just trying to get out of embarrassing yourself at charades," Simon said.

Grace swatted him on the upper arm, and it struck her how familial the gesture was. So much so that she didn't make eye contact with anyone as she pushed her chair back and stood.

"Come on, Evan," she said. "We've both got busy days tomorrow."

Merline followed them to the door. She placed a gentle hand on Grace's arm. "Thank you for staying for dinner." She cast a loving glance at Evan.

Grace smiled because she really did like Merline, had often dreamed of having someone like her for a mother. If only things had turned out differently between Nathan and

Grace, she might have been. She pushed that thought away before it brought back the old sadness.

"It was a wonderful meal. I think I could have eaten half of that cake myself."

"You're welcome back anytime."

Grace nodded and ushered Evan out the door into the night. She had to distance herself from the warm comfort of the Teague family, of what a family should be, before she caved and begged to stay, to be brought into the fold. The slim chance for that had passed long ago.

Hadn't it?

Yes. That kiss was an aberration, nothing more.

Albeit an aberration she couldn't purge from her memory.

When they reached the cabin, Evan grasped her hand. He was doing that less and less as he got older, so she knew something was bothering him.

"Are you okay, Mom?"

She sank onto the edge of the leather ottoman. "Yes, honey, I'm fine. It was just a tiring day, that's all. You don't need to worry about me anymore, okay?"

"You're sure?"

The worry in his eyes broke her heart. She

hated what her illness had put him through. "I'm sure. Now, off to bed with you. I won't have you falling asleep on top of a horse tomorrow."

He smiled. "That wouldn't happen."

"Not if you get enough sleep." She gestured toward the bedroom.

Evan kissed her on the cheek and headed off to bed. Grace sat in the same spot for countless minutes, letting random thoughts flit in and out of her mind. More often than was safe for her heart, she relived the kiss she'd shared with Nathan beneath the stars. She could no longer deny that a very large part of her still wanted Nathan, would be too easily tempted into thinking that he wanted her for her alone.

It was a nice fantasy, but that's all she could allow it to be. How could she ever be sure Nathan wasn't toying with her feelings to gain access to his son? He didn't strike her as that type of man, not one raised by Hank and Merline, but she couldn't be one hundred percent certain.

That was her problem, wasn't it? Everything had to be concrete, in her control, totally without uncertainty. Only life had an annoying way of wrecking all of that.

Despite her assertion that she was tired, and

she was, she didn't make a move toward the bedroom. Normally, the warmth and safety of a well-appointed room was a balm, but tonight the walls seemed too close. Once she was sure Evan was tucked into bed and sleeping soundly, she stepped outside and returned to the picnic table that looked down on the main part of the ranch. Everything that cluster of buildings, and the people inside them, represented made her heart ache with longing. She didn't allow herself to miss having a family often because it hurt too much, but tonight she let the tears flow. So much emotion was roiling inside her that she had to let some of it out.

Footsteps crunched the gravel of the drive that circled past all of the cabins. She glanced over her shoulder and could barely make out the shape of a tall man coming closer. Her heart leapt until the man stepped onto the porch of her cabin and the light from inside revealed it to be Barrett Farnsley. He was a nice man, but she was in no mood to talk to him. When he knocked on the door and stepped back to wait, she sat perfectly still, hoping he wouldn't see her.

He didn't knock a second time, and Grace wasn't sure she breathed, at least not audibly, until he was back in his own cabin. She wrapped her arms around herself and stared up into the sky. Were her parents still the same people they'd always been? Had any sliver of regret entered their hearts at how they'd treated her and Evan?

Grace shook her head when she tried to imagine her mother making a decadent strawberry cake or playing charades or even painting wildflowers in a field. When she tried to imagine her siblings as more like the Teague brothers, it proved impossible. Why was she the only one who'd wanted more from life?

The sound of footsteps broke into her musings again. Had Barrett finally seen her? She slowly glanced over her shoulder, but realized immediately that the man walking toward her wasn't Barrett Farnsley. And it was too late to make a break for the cabin and feign sleep. He'd seen her.

"Are you okay?" Nathan asked as he stepped close.

"Everyone keeps asking me that."

"Maybe we have good reason."

She sighed, more tired mentally than physically. "Just doing some ill-advised looking back."

"Your family or a boy who was a big jerk in high school?"

For some reason, the way he said it caused her to laugh a little. "A bit of both."

"Would it help the jerk's case if he brought you cake now?" Nathan held up a plastic container. "I could tell you liked it tonight."

"You're trying to buy me off with dessert?"

"Um, yes. Is it working?"

Damn, he was charming. He'd had a bit of that charm in high school, but it'd been overshadowed by teenage stupidity at the time. He'd grown into it, just like he'd grown into that awesome body of his.

Grace shifted her gaze away from him. "Maybe a little."

He placed the container on the table next to her then walked around to the other side and sat beside her. "Then I'll have to make daily runs to Mehlerhaus Bakery to bring all manner of sweets."

Grace almost let the comment pass, but instead looked at Nathan's strong profile. "What are you doing?"

He looked at her. "Just trying to be your friend, get to know you again."

"You didn't really know me the first time, Nathan." She knew it sounded bitter, but evidently when emotions started flowing out she had little control over them.

"Then I'll get to know you for the first time."

He wasn't backing down, and the wall of resistance she'd erected started to crumble. She stared down at the lights of the ranch, saw a set of headlights come on as an engine started.

"Guess the charades must be over," Nathan said.

"So you all went ahead and played?"

"Mom got it in her head to play. No getting out of it."

Grace almost wished she'd stayed, at least to witness the entire family together, laughing and joking. "You have a great family," she said.

He nodded. "Yeah. I think I'll keep them."

Grace smiled.

Nathan shifted and let his hands hang loosely between his knees. "Do you ever speak to your family?"

"No, not since the day they kicked me out. They had their chance, more than once."

"I can't imagine being that alone."

"At times, it was so freeing, so refreshing, but others it was just damned hard. If it hadn't been for Emily, I don't know what I would have done."

"I've been doing a lot of thinking. There's a part of me that's probably always going to be angry that I've missed so much with Evan, and I have no intention of missing any more."

Grace's nerves crackled and her stomach knotted. What was he saying?

"But I'm sorry you felt you couldn't come to me," he said. "I know why. If I could go back and knock some sense into my younger self, I'd do it."

Grace let out a small, wary sigh. "I appreciate the sentiment. In hindsight, I know I could have handled things better than I did. I dreamed about telling you the truth, that everything would be okay, but fear is a powerful deterrent. Then I thought that maybe you were married with other children, that maybe you wouldn't want to be saddled with one you didn't know. I thought that if you'd just agree to take Evan if anything happened to me, that would be enough."

"You know I will. He's a good kid, my kid."

Grace sighed in relief. "Thank you."

"Did you really doubt I'd agree?"

"I didn't know. I mean, this not knowing each other thing goes both ways. I was scared of what I might find when I met you again."

"And yet you came anyway. Why?"

Grace heard some of his frustration slip out. She resisted the urge to get to her feet and put some distance between Nathan and herself. "I told you."

"Yes, but I think there's something specific that triggered this."

Why was she resisting telling him? He'd already said he'd take care of Evan. If she'd ever doubted her son would find love here, the past few days had erased that particular fear.

"Why does Evan look at you sometimes like he has to take care of you?"

Grace propped her elbow on her knee and dropped her forehead into her palm. "Because he thought I was going to die."

"What?"

She lifted her head and looked him in the eye for the first time since his appearance. "Because I had cancer and had to go through chemo. He saw me when I was at my absolute worst. To be honest, I'm not sure I would have made it through without him to live for."

"Oh, my God, Grace. Why didn't you come to me sooner? I could have helped."

"Because I was too busy hanging over toilets and pulling out clumps of my hair."

Nathan reached over and grasped her shoulders, turned her toward him. "Are you okay now?"

She nodded, blinked back the tears that

sprang to her eyes at what sounded like genuine concern on his part. "I got a clean bill of health about a month ago. But what I went through already scarred Evan, and I hate that I did that to him."

"You didn't get sick on purpose. Stop being so hard on yourself."

Her chin quivered, and the tears broke free and ran down her cheeks. "I'm so scared it'll come back and I won't get to see Evan grow up."

Nathan pulled her into his arms, against his warm body, and for once she let herself cry without holding back, allowing herself to be comforted.

Grace seemed so small wrapped in his arms. He couldn't remember if she'd felt this way when he'd held her at that party, or if he'd grown and she was smaller because of her recent illness.

God, cancer. Hadn't she been through enough in her life already without having that thrown at her, too? He hated himself for being part of the cause for her unwillingness to contact him sooner. No matter how long it took him, he'd atone for that. And make her believe that she didn't have to be alone anymore.

Something about that thought shook him, scared him a little. What exactly did he feel for her? Yes, she was beautiful, was the mother of his son, had been through more than one person should have to face. But apart from all of that, how did he, Nathan the man, feel about Grace, the woman?

She tried to pull away, but he only let her go so far, still managing to keep an arm around her shoulders.

"I'm sorry I blubbered all over you." She looked up at him, really looked him in the eye. It felt like the first time she'd truly done so without immediately averting her gaze.

He reached up and wiped away a tear at the edge of her eye. "I don't mind. You needed it."

"You're right, I did. Sometimes I don't realize how much I bottle things up to keep Evan from seeing them. He's worried enough, too much for someone his age. I want him to be happy and carefree."

"Like he's been this week?"

She stiffened and tried to pull away again. Nathan let her but clasped one of her hands between his. "Grace, I'm not trying to pressure you or cause more upheaval in your life. I'm just putting it out there, something to think about. I had a good life growing up here, and if Evan could spend at least part of his time here, too… I think he'd enjoy it."

Grace surprised him by placing her other hand on top of his. "You might be right. I see how in love with this place he already is."

"And that scares you."

She nodded. "I lost him once, and he nearly lost me. Call it irrational, but I'm afraid that the next time something comes between us, it'll be for good."

"I wouldn't do that."

She met his gaze. "Maybe you wouldn't mean to."

He looked hard into her eyes, trying to figure out what was really bothering her. It hit him the moment she bit her bottom lip, a gesture identical to the one he'd seen from Evan.

"You can't think he'd want to be with me more." Nathan squeezed Grace's hand. "You're his mother, the person who has always been there for him."

"And a boy yearns for a father. Plus, you're the embodiment of everything Evan thinks is cool. How can I compete with that?"

"It's not a competition."

"I'm just not ready to make that step, Nathan. Call me fragile, hard, selfish, whatever you like—"

Nathan placed his fingers gently against her lips. "Stop. We don't have to talk about this any more right now."

He'd give anything to be able to douse that fear he could see in her eyes despite the darkness of the night. For her sake, for Evan's. And, yes, for his own. Before he realized what he was doing, he let his thumb slide over her bottom lip. His heart thudded against his chest. When was the last time a woman had caused him to feel light-headed?

"I want to kiss you right now, but I'm afraid you'll take it the wrong way."

He expected her to retreat, but she sat still, looking up at him. The fear in her eyes gave way to something else, something that he thought might be a yearning that matched his own. He didn't wait for her to tell him that it wasn't a good idea. When his lips touched hers, the soft, slow kiss wasn't enough. He pulled her close and deepened the kiss. She moaned into his mouth, fueling the hunger building inside him. His memories of the one time they'd been together were admittedly hazy, but he was certain there hadn't been a true fire like this involved.

Damn if he wasn't in danger of falling for Grace Cameron, and falling hard. The realization hit him like a rogue lightning bolt out of the sky. But he couldn't tell her. She wouldn't believe him, might in fact take Evan and run as fast as she could back to her life in Arkansas. Then he might be forced to take steps that would hurt her even more. He'd been telling her the truth when he'd said he had no intention of missing any more of Evan's life.

Though it pained him to do so, he was the one to pull back. "I think I better let you get some rest."

She looked suddenly embarrassed, and he couldn't let her doubt what had passed between them. He kissed her fingers.

"Not that this isn't very nice."

He'd bet money that he would see a pretty blush on her cheeks if there were more light.

They both slid off the table and headed toward the cabin. Unable to resist, he wrapped her hand in his and was surprised by how comfortable, how right it felt. She either liked it as well or was too tired to resist.

When they reached the front steps of the cabin, she held up the plastic container. "Thanks for the cake."

He ran his thumb across the top of her hand. "Thanks for being honest with me. I want you to know, no matter where things stand at the end of the week, you can come to me for help. I don't want you going through any more bad stuff alone."

Grace bit her lip again, and for a moment he thought she might cry more tears. Instead, she lifted to her tiptoes and kissed him. It was quick and sweet, but it was a kiss she initiated. He watched as she hurried into the cabin. Even after she closed the door behind her, he stared at it until a wide smile spread across his face.

He was going to win that woman if it was the last thing he did.

Chapter Eleven

Grace was fairly certain that she spent equal parts of the next day working on plans for Merline's gallery and thinking about Nathan. Drawing sketches and reliving his kiss of the night before. Meeting with a contractor and remembering how she'd kissed him back. Selecting furnishings and daydreaming about being in his arms again and how she was dangerously close to believing they could start over, maybe have a relationship.

The ringing of her phone startled her from a fantasy of Nathan feeding her some of that delicious strawberry cake. A glance at the display showed it was Emily. She hit the button to answer.

"Hey, Em."

"Hey, yourself. How's the cowboying going?"

"Evan's having a great time."

"And you?"

"Good." Grace was glad it wasn't a video call. She didn't want to explain the sudden rush of blood to her face.

"Well, I'm about to make things even better."

"Let me guess, you won a new copy machine."

Emily laughed. "No, but I'm feeling the biggest, baddest copier just around the corner."

Grace's heartbeat sped up. "We got the job?"

"We got the job."

"Yes!" Grace squealed and did a little dance. The Franklin Mountain Lodge was their biggest project yet, one that could catapult their business to the next level and provide more security for her and Evan as well as Emily.

A flash of Nathan offering a different kind of security caused her to still. No, she couldn't let maybes trump a sure thing.

"They've asked for a meeting next Friday. If all goes well, we'll sign the paperwork and be official."

"That's great."

"Is something wrong?"

Grace stared out the window at the light glinting off the lake, at the bluebonnets waving in a cooler-than-normal breeze. "No, why?"

"I don't know. You sounded hesitant or something."

"Sorry. It's just a nice surprise. I'm stunned, I guess."

"Why? We are the dynamic duo, after all."

Grace laughed at the nickname they'd adopted for themselves when they'd received the top grade on a group design project in college, the one that now graced their business, Dynamic Duo Designs. "True."

"Is something else going on?"

Grace slumped into the lawn chair she'd found on the back patio of the gallery building. "Nothing that I can't handle once I'm hundreds of miles from here."

"Is Nathan giving you a hard time?"

"No, not exactly."

"Then what, exactly?"

Grace closed her eyes. "Those feelings that I had for him when we were in high school? Well, they might not have gone anywhere."

"O-kay. Does he know that?"

"I'm guessing yes, based on the kissing."

Emily squealed so loudly that Grace had to pull the phone away from her ear. When she brought it back, she said, "Good Lord, woman. I'd like to retain my hearing in that ear."

"What, you tell me you're kissing Evan's father and you don't expect me to squeal? You know me better than that."

"Trust me, it surprised me, too."

"Well, how was it?"

"Honestly? Fantastic. After all this time, he still makes me melt."

Emily was quiet for a moment. "What does this mean, Grace?"

"Don't worry, Em. It's just a little leftover flirtation or something. It's not like we've fallen in love and are going to live happily ever after amidst the bluebonnets." But as she said it, a deep, burning need for exactly that washed through her.

"You sure about that?"

"You know my life is there."

"If you say so."

Grace didn't know what to make of Emily's reaction. It sounded like a mixture of worry that Grace wasn't coming back and potential matchmaking *a la* Laney. She wondered how fast those two would be on the phone to each other when Laney found out what had happened.

They spent a few more minutes discussing the details of their upcoming meeting and all the activities Evan was taking part in, but Grace didn't mention the gallery or her hand in it. She didn't want to give Emily more reason to believe Grace might be bailing on her, but it still felt wrong to keep it from her oldest and best friend. She told herself she'd tell Em about it after she got home, when the gallery, Merline, Blue Falls and Nathan were far away.

The good mood she'd enjoyed all day dampened at that thought. Suddenly, the hours until she and Evan had to leave seemed way too few.

"I gotta run. The office line is ringing," Emily said.

"Okay, bye."

After she hung up, Grace continued sitting in the chair. Her natural inclination at this point would be to chastise herself for letting down her guard and starting something with Nathan that could go nowhere. But for some reason, that wasn't what she felt. True, her time here was short, but that only made her want to enjoy it more.

Sometime during the past few days, the dread that had been sitting on her shoulder, whispering all kinds of negative scenarios into her ear from the moment she'd decided to confess the truth to Nathan, had dissipated like morning fog. Slow and gradual so that she didn't notice until it was gone.

After everything she'd been through, she deserved to enjoy something. And she enjoyed being with Nathan. As long as she went in with her eyes wide open and knowing not to let it go too far, she was just going to see what happened over the next few days.

She gathered her notes, locked the building and headed back to the ranch. The closer she got, the more the excitement at seeing Nathan again built inside her. When she parked at the ranch, she immediately spotted him helping Juan lead the horses from the corral back to their stalls. She entered the barn from the opposite end, her pulse picking up even more when he saw her and smiled.

"You had a long day," he said.

"Lots to do, now that your mom has signed the papers. It's a bit like being caught up in a whirlwind."

"If I know Mom, she'll have the place up and running in a week."

Grace hated that she wouldn't be around for the opening. Maybe when Evan was older, they could come back. Perhaps she'd even get up the nerve to reveal the truth to him and trust that he wouldn't abandon her at the first opportunity.

She shook off that line of thought, remembering that she wanted to focus on the present. "Evan in the house?"

"Yes, he and the rest of the kids are having freshly baked cookies and a *Toy Story* marathon."

Grace laughed. "Was that Evan's idea?"

"No, Cheyenne's. But I think she might have done it because of Evan."

"Hmm, determined little girl."

"Not wasting time going after what she wants."

Grace met Nathan's eyes, and a thrill zipped through her at the intensity in that gaze. Could he possibly be having thoughts similar to her own?

He led one of the horses into its stall then closed the door and motioned for her to follow him out of the barn. "Do you have plans for tonight?"

"No, not really."

"What would you say if I suggested a picnic, just you and me?"

Her heart fluttered. "Yes."

His eyes widened. "That was easier than I thought."

She couldn't help smiling. "I feel good today, and I think I have you to thank for that."

He raised an eyebrow and gave her a rakish grin. "Really?"

"Don't get too cocky about it, though."

He laughed, and she loved the sound, could imagine listening to it every day without it getting old.

"All I meant was that I feel better having everything out in the open." Well, not everything, but she couldn't divulge how she was pretty sure she was halfway in love with him all over again. How she'd maybe never stopped loving him despite how he'd acted in the days after they'd made love.

His expression grew serious. "You're really okay? The doctors got everything?"

She nodded. "Trust me, I made them check more than once."

"I'm glad."

They were simple words, but something about the way he said them, so full of a gut-deep truth she never expected, made her go warm all over.

"Wait here," he said. "I'll be back in five minutes."

"I need to tell Evan where I'm going."

"Don't worry. I'll tell Mom, and she can tell him. They're probably only halfway into the first movie anyway."

"Okay." She supressed a very girlish giggle as she watched Nathan walk toward the back door that led to the kitchen. She hoped no one could see her because she took the opportunity to fully appreciate the nice things the man did for a pair of jeans. He gave them purpose.

This jittery excitement was how she'd felt that night when she'd crawled out of her bedroom window to meet him at that party. Only this time, she didn't have to worry about getting caught.

A man of his word, he was back within five minutes, a wicker picnic basket in hand and a blanket draped over his arm. After they slid into his truck, he headed up a road that led off in the opposite direction from the cabins.

"Where does this road go?"

He glanced at her, a knowing smile on his face. "It's a surprise."

A few minutes and several winding turns later, he pulled up in front of a small house, about twice the size of the cabins. It dawned on her where he'd taken her.

"This is your home?"

"Yes, but that's not what I wanted to show you." He got out of the truck, taking the basket and blanket with him. She opened her door and joined him. He took her hand and led her around the edge of the house and down a path that led into a wooded area.

When they emerged on the other side, Grace gasped. Far below in the distance lay Blue Falls, the lake, and the falls. "Oh, Nathan, it's beautiful." She let go of his hand and walked to the edge of the ridge.

"I thought you might like it."

She looked over her shoulder at him. "I'm surprised you didn't build your house here, where you could see this every time you looked out."

"I didn't want to mar the view of the hills from town."

Grace turned more fully toward him. "You really aren't the same person you used to be."

"I'm guessing that's a good thing."

"In some ways. Maybe we've just both grown up."

He nodded and stared out toward the lake for a few seconds. "Well, I don't know about you, but I'm hungry." He placed the basket to the side then spread out the blanket.

Grace sat as Nathan started pulling food

out of the basket: ham-and-cheese sandwiches on thick sourdough bread, homemade potato salad, a jar of baby gherkins.

"Hey, these are my favorite kind of pickles," she said as she scooped a gherkin out of the jar.

Nathan smiled. "Evan might have said something about that while looking in the fridge."

"I hope he's not making a nuisance of himself."

"Not at all. Mom loves feeding him."

Grace took a bite of the pickle and considered whether she really wanted the answer to the question rolling around in her head. "Does your family think I'm awful for not telling Evan the truth?"

Nathan shook his head. "Not awful, but we all want you to reconsider. I think you're underestimating Evan."

"You say that after only knowing him a few days."

"Sometimes it's easier to see something if you're more removed."

Grace drew up her knees and wrapped her arms around them. "Is this why you brought me out here, to hound me about telling Evan the truth?"

"No. I wanted to spend time with you."

Grace met Nathan's eyes, tried to see beyond the surface. She wished, so much, that she could take him at face value and not worry about ulterior motives.

"Listen, no matter when Evan gets told the truth, you and I are going to stay in touch. Don't you think we ought to get to know each other better?"

She considered his words for several seconds before nodding.

"Now, how about we eat and enjoy the sunset?"

Grace accepted one of the sandwiches and a small container of potato salad. She watched as the sun dipped lower toward the horizon, casting a gorgeous orange glow across the surface of the lake.

"All the times I came out to the ranch to tutor you, I never knew it held so many beautiful spots. Here, the meadow where I found your mom painting." Or maybe all of her attention had been directed toward the boy who needed tutoring.

"Now you see why it means so much to Mom and Dad. This place gets in your blood."

"I don't think it's just your parents in love with this land."

"There was a time I thought I would leave, after I finished school. You know, the whole

'I'm going to be different than my parents' thing."

"Oh, yeah, I know it well." It was the first time she'd ever been able to find an ounce of humor in the division between her parents and herself. Maybe she was simply finished dwelling on it, ready to leave it firmly in the past.

"When it came time to actually make the decision, I couldn't do it. I couldn't imagine anywhere else I'd want to be more. Ryan left for a while, but came back. Simon has his job in law enforcement, but he can't break all the ties, either."

"That type of attachment seems so foreign to me. Even when we lived here, I didn't feel it. I felt I was always apart from everything and everyone around me."

"I think I probably knew that."

"Is that why you asked me to that party? Pity?"

"The truth? I'm not sure. Maybe. I mean, I thought you were kind of pretty, but you know how stupid boys can be. I was a prime example. I remember that I didn't think you'd actually come to the party."

It shouldn't have hurt, especially considering all the worse things she'd lived through, but it did.

"It wasn't meant to be cruel, but I'm still not proud of it."

She stared at the weave of the blanket between her feet. "It was a long time ago."

"I'm still sorry."

"I guess we both have things to be sorry for."

"I suppose."

They ate in silence for a couple of minutes, Grace working through feelings both current and past.

"I just have one other question, and then I want to leave our past in the past and move forward," she said.

"Okay."

"Why did you make love to me that night?"

Nathan let out a long, slow sigh, picked at a fuzzball on the blanket. "I'd had too much to drink."

Grace's heart constricted, but she plunged forward. "Was that the only reason? I just happened to be handy?"

"No." He shook his head as if trying to clear cobwebs. "You were nice, even if you were shy. Pretty, though I'm ashamed to say I would have never admitted that to my friends. If circumstances had been different..." He shrugged. "I honestly don't know."

Grace swallowed past the lump forming in her throat. What had she expected him to say? That he had harbored a secret love for her, too? Her life had never been a fairy tale, so why she'd thought maybe it would start now, she had no idea.

"Why did you let me? I wasn't so drunk that I wouldn't have stopped if you'd asked me."

"Because I was in love with you."

"And you expected what, that having sex would make me love you back?"

Grace shifted where she sat and battled the urge to walk away. Maybe catharsis from the past was way overrated. Nathan reached over and grasped her hand, a gentle gesture she couldn't imagine his younger self offering.

"Probably somewhere deep down, that's exactly what I hoped," she said. "I wanted to matter to someone as something more than a free babysitter or another body to work and bring home money."

Nathan's hand tightened a bit on hers, not enough to hurt but enough that she realized her words affected him.

"Your tutoring money, they took it?"

"Yes. We weren't allowed to have money of our own. It was expected for us to work and help support the family."

She glanced at Nathan in time to see his jaw tighten. It warmed her heart to see that he was angry on her behalf.

"It doesn't matter now," she said. "I've come to realize that hanging on to all the old anger doesn't do anyone any good. They will never change, but I can. Them tossing me out was probably the best thing they could have done for me. I got Evan back, an education, a good life. I've conquered cancer, for goodness' sake. If that's not something to be happy about, I don't know what is."

When she finished speaking, she noticed a different look on Nathan's face. It startled her because it looked a lot like how she'd wanted him to look at her when they were teenagers.

"You're an amazing woman, Grace Cameron."

She felt the blush crawl up her neck and fill her face, so she tried to hide it by taking another bite of potato salad and directing her attention to where the sun now sat three-quarters of the way below the horizon.

"You ever notice how fast the sun seems to set when it gets to the horizon? You can almost see it actually move," she said.

"Yeah."

The silence between them grew awkward,

at least for Grace. She searched for something to say, but came up with nothing.

"Grace?"

"Hmm?"

"You think we could start over?"

"I told you, it's all in the past now. No sense in rehashing it again."

He scooted closer to her, seated himself so that he was facing her. "That's not what I mean."

The feel of Nathan's hand caressing her cheek caused her breath to lose its way, flustered by an unexpected turn. "What are you doing?"

"What I should have a long time ago." He kissed her as he slid his fingers through her hair to the back of her head, pulling her closer.

There was something different about this kiss, something deeper. Her natural defenses threatened, but they were overshadowed by a swell of joy. Whatever happened afterward, she was going to indulge in this moment. So she kissed him back with all the love she'd once held for him, maybe still did.

He wanted her. With every part of his body, Nathan wanted Grace. And at least for the moment, she seemed to want him, too.

The sun was long gone, and soon the last light of the day would join it. In the fading light, he lay Grace back on the blanket and kissed her more deeply. When her hands ran up his back into his hair, flames licked at his body. His heart thudded wildly, and other parts of him came to life.

He slid his hands underneath her T-shirt, up her slender rib cage to the bottom of her bra. Somewhere in the back of his mind, he expected her to protest. When she didn't, he edged even higher and caressed the part of her breast above her bra.

"You're so soft," he whispered against her lips.

"And you're not," she said, her breath ragged enough to tell him she was feeling just as hot and bothered as he was.

He laughed. "Is that a problem?"

"No."

Nathan nibbled at her ear. "Good to know."

He couldn't remember the last time he'd kissed a woman so much, or when it hadn't been nearly enough. When Grace's hands found their way up the back of his shirt, he was the one to moan.

She stilled where she lay halfway beneath him.

"Are you okay?" he asked.

Her big, beautiful eyes stared up at him. "I know I should stop, but I don't want to."

"Me, neither." He kissed her, lightly this time. "You said it, we're different people now. It's not like before."

She didn't say anything for so long he wondered if this entire outing had been a mistake.

"What is this about?" she asked.

It took him a couple of moments to realize what must be tormenting her mind. He caressed her cheek. "I can assure you this has absolutely nothing to do with Evan."

"You're sure?"

He edged closer so that she could feel exactly what she was doing to him.

"Grace, if we had never had a child, I would still want to make love to you right now. And I'm fully prepared to show you how much."

Chapter Twelve

A week ago, Nathan's words might have scared Grace. But now? Every part of her body was screaming, "Yes!" Everything was out in the open. He swore this had nothing to do with Evan, and even if it did she wouldn't let it affect her decision. But she wanted Nathan, wanted to make love to him when she wasn't a shy, moony-eyed, sheltered girl.

He slid his hand under her bra, and the feel of his calloused palm rubbing across the tip of her breast made her gasp. His lips blazed a trail from her ear down her neck.

She guided him back to her mouth and kissed him so deeply she thought she might become a part of him. Her hands found their way to the buttons on his shirt and started flicking them open. As soon as they were free of their confines, she pushed his shirt apart and ran her hands over his chest.

"You're killing me," he said, his breath warm against her wet lips.

She smiled. "I doubt that."

Not to be outdone, he tugged at the bottom of her shirt and had it off her so quickly it could qualify as a magic trick. Before she could wrangle her whirling thoughts, he'd undone her bra and disposed of it, as well.

For a moment, a sliver of worry taunted her, but then his warm, wonderful mouth captured one of her breasts and she forgot everything but the tugging, aching sensation radiating out from her breast to every part of her body.

Caution and common sense took flight as Grace lost herself to the sensations coming at her from all directions. As she fully indulged in these new feelings—ones she hadn't even approached when she and Nathan had made love before—the rest of their clothes joined her shirt and bra.

Grace ran her fingers over the taut, warm skin of his shoulders and back. Heavens, he was beautiful to behold. She lay with Nathan, skin to skin, a dream come to real, breathing life. A shiver ran through her.

"Are you cold?" he asked as he kissed the curve of her jaw.

"Not in the least."

He chuckled and shifted in a way that made his desire even more obvious. A little gasp escaped her just as her gaze met his.

"Is this okay? I know I'm late asking that question, but I should have asked it the first time."

His words, his honest concern touched her in a place so deep she hadn't known it'd existed until that moment.

"Yes. This time, I think we both want it."

"I know I do. And this time, it's not alcohol or stupid teenage hormones talking." He ran the tip of his forefinger across her lips. "It's all me."

Grace slid her hand slowly down Nathan's back to his hips, applying a needy pressure there. "It's not *all* you."

Nathan captured her mouth again, and Grace gave herself over to pure sensation. There would be time enough to think later, but not now.

His hands found all the right places to send her into higher and higher planes of enjoyment until finally it wasn't enough. She whispered into his ear. "Make love to me, Nathan."

"With pleasure." It was part human response, part animal growl.

She grasped his shoulders as he spread her legs with his knee and proceeded to fulfill her command.

Making love to Nathan again had blown all of Grace's fantasies away. But it was the gentle and protective way he'd wrapped the blanket around them and how he now held her close to him that had Grace on the verge of shedding happy tears.

"Please tell me you're not regretting this," Nathan said, his breath stirring her hair.

"I'm not." Her voice sounded choked, and Nathan noticed. He leaned back and lifted her face toward his.

"Are you about to cry?"

"I'm trying not to."

"What did I do wrong?" He sounded so at a loss that she caressed his cheek with all the love she was feeling but hadn't spoken aloud.

"Nothing. If these tears fall, they'll be happy ones." She considered the wisdom of her next words before saying them. "I've never felt so wonderful, so…safe in my entire life."

A potent mixture of pride and happiness lit up his face. Just the idea that she could make him happy had her thoughts shooting off in directions she'd never dared consider. Thoughts that included a future with Nathan as more than just Evan's parent. She had to rein in those crazy notions before she set herself up for more hurt. She was going home soon, back to her life and responsibilities. She burrowed closer to him as that reality threatened to turn her happy tears into ones of sorrow.

"I'm glad," Nathan said. "I'm feeling pretty damn wonderful myself."

He kissed her forehead, which led to kisses on her eyelids, cheeks and then mouth. The hot and heady sensations started to build, and insistent caresses led to them making love again.

"Nathan Teague, you are trying to render me completely useless," she said afterward as she waited for her heart to slow.

He nibbled on her ear. "You are far from useless, Grace Cameron. In fact, I can think of all kinds of fun uses for you."

It was almost scary how happy his words made her feel. She wondered if she was dreaming, though she couldn't imagine a dream feeling this real.

She snuggled closer to him, trying not to

think about the moment when they'd have to leave this spot and the feel of each other to return to reality. Trying not to think about how soon she'd be leaving Nathan behind again, and how her heart might cleave right down the scar caused by the last time it had broken over him.

She ran her hand across his chest, memorizing the texture and contours. In the quiet of the night, she allowed herself to wonder what might happen if she told Evan the truth. Would he understand? Would he want to move to Texas? Would Nathan, having achieved the desired relationship with his son, not be interested in her anymore?

Grace closed her eyes and told herself not to be so skeptical. He'd said what they'd shared had nothing to do with Evan, and his words had rung with truth. But what had tonight been? Simple desire? Was she okay with that?

No, she wasn't. She might tell herself this evening was just two adults enjoying themselves with no promises, might even want it to be true, but deep down that wasn't who she was. She was a falling in love and forever kind of girl.

She shifted away from Nathan. "We need to get going." And she didn't want Nathan's family getting ideas about what was happening, that it might change her plans.

Nathan grabbed her around the waist and pulled her back toward him. "Stay."

Grace placed her palm against his bare chest, but the feel of him sapped her intention to push herself away. "Evan will be wondering where I am."

Nathan placed his hand over hers. "I'm not talking about right here, right now. I want you to stay here at the ranch longer. You just got here."

"I can't do that. Evan has school."

"Not for another week."

Obviously, her son had spilled that his spring break was two weeks and not one.

"I have to get back to work."

"You've been doing some of your work here. Can't you continue that for a few more days?"

Why did he have to tempt her so? "I have an important meeting coming up. We're about to land our biggest client yet. It could be an important turning point for our business."

Nathan released her hand and ran his fingertips softly over the swell of her breast. "What day is your meeting?"

She closed her eyes and through a herculean

effort pulled her thoughts away from the feel of his fingers. "Next Friday."

"Then you can spend a few more days here. You can work on the gallery. Evan can spend more time playing cowboy without all the other visitors here."

"Nathan—"

He placed those wonderful fingertips against her lips. "Our deal still stands. I just want more time, Grace." His gaze met hers, and what she saw there made her flush with a glorious warmth. "And not just with Evan."

Nathan lowered his mouth to hers, and she dissolved under the power of the kiss.

"Say yes," he said against her lips.

"Nathan."

He kissed his way down her neck. "Say yes."

"I can't—"

His mouth captured a breast with a hunger that had her bowing her back to get closer. "Say yes," he said again, his voice a sexy growl against the tip of her breast.

"Yes." Oh, mercy, yes.

Nathan stood off to the side of the group of guests he'd led up the trail the next morning, but he only had eyes for one. Grace looked almost as sexy in a pair of well-worn jeans and a

T-shirt as she had wearing nothing but a blanket and his arms around her.

He'd had the damndest time all morning keeping from constantly turning around in his saddle to watch her riding beside their son. And when he'd seen Barrett Farnsley riding beside her, saying something that made her laugh, he'd ground his teeth together.

But then she'd met his gaze and the memory of what they'd shared the night before was right there, shining in her beautiful eyes. She'd gifted him with a shy, knowing smile even as Farnsley continued speaking.

"You sure that's a good idea?" Simon asked from beside him.

"What?"

Simon nodded toward where Grace was sitting next to Evan on a log eating a sandwich. "Grace. And don't even try to deny something happened. I've got eyes."

Nathan didn't say anything. What was going on between him and Grace was no one's business but theirs.

"Has she changed her mind?"

Nathan thought about not answering, but he knew his brother. Simon wasn't going anywhere until he got some answers.

"No, but just give it some time." She had to

see he'd be a good father, that maybe he and she could continue what they'd started.

"I'm not sure some good rolls in the hay are going to change things."

Nathan whirled toward his brother, anger shooting to the surface with amazing swiftness. "That isn't what this is about."

"It's not?"

"No." He wasn't sure exactly what was happening between them, but he'd told the truth the night before. If Evan wasn't even in the picture, he'd still want her. The potency of how much he wanted her surprised him, but he wasn't going to fight it.

"Listen, I like Grace. I'm just saying that she made it clear she wasn't coming here to stay, right? It seemed like that resolve was pretty solid, not something that's going to disappear in a few days no matter what's going on between you two."

"And your point?"

Simon took off his hat and scratched his head. "Maybe you should see what your options are in case she does as she plans, and goes back home without telling Evan you're his father. You have rights."

Nathan stared hard at his brother. "What, you want me to take her to court or something?" The more he got to know her, the worse that idea sounded.

"Not necessarily. Just determine the options, that's all."

"Thanks for the advice, but I'm good." But as Nathan stalked away, Simon's words started speaking to the common sense side of him, the side that wanted to make sure he had a relationship with his son before he lost any more time.

Maybe he'd consult an attorney just to see where he stood, as long as Grace didn't find out. He still hoped he could convince her to give his vision of the future a try.

He made his way across the site they sometimes used for overnight camping trips, skirting the fire ring set in the midst of several segments of logs being used as benches where everyone ate their lunches. When he got close to Grace and Evan, it hit him how used to seeing them every day he'd become in such a short time. He couldn't imagine waking up in the morning knowing they were hundreds of miles away with no guarantee of seeing them again. He wondered at what moment keeping Grace near became as important as making sure he maintained contact with Evan.

"How'd you like the ride up here?" he asked Evan as he drew close to him.

"It was great," Evan said around a mouth full of sandwich.

"Don't talk with your mouth full," Grace said.

"Okay," Evan mumbled, trying not to show his food.

Nathan laughed and shifted his attention to Grace. "How about you?"

"It was beautiful, but I have a feeling I'm not going to be able to walk tomorrow."

Nathan had a vision of other reasons she might be left unable to walk, and he got the impression she could read his mind when she blushed and lowered her eyes. Man, he wanted her right now, but he didn't think dragging her off to have his way with her was a particularly wise idea.

But the image of doing exactly that plagued him during the entire ride back down to the stables. After everyone dismounted, the tired guests turned over the horses and made their way back to their cars. Grace held on to Dolly's and Hazel's reins as Evan ran off with Cheyenne and the Farnsley boys to see a litter of kittens that had been born that morning while they'd all been on the trail ride.

Grace guided Dolly and Hazel into the barn behind Nathan and his two charges. He couldn't get the horses turned over to Abel and Juan fast enough. As he and Grace exited the barn, he grabbed her and pulled her around the edge of the building into the shaded area facing the open pastures. Once they were out of sight of everyone else, he backed her against the side of the barn and lowered his mouth to hers.

She tasted like the nectarine he'd seen her eating at lunch, sweet and juicy. And the curves of her body pressed against him sent his hands exploring.

"I've wanted to do that all day," he said when he came up for air.

"Nathan," she breathed against his mouth. "Evan is just inside."

"He's busy." He kissed her again, and she relented and kissed him back with a fervor that illustrated just how much Grace had changed. He might not remember everything from that night when they'd hooked up, but he did remember how timid and unsure she'd been. Now she seemed like a woman who knew exactly what she wanted and just had to convince herself to allow it to happen.

He shoved his hands under her shirt and up over the soft skin covering her ribs. Never had he felt as though a woman was a drug to which he could so easily get addicted. He had to fight not to strip her naked and take her right there against the side of the barn.

He broke the kiss, retrieved his hands and backed away. "I'm sorry. I don't know what's gotten into me." He took a couple of steps toward the fence. "I shouldn't be treating you like that."

She was silent except for the sound of trying to catch her breath. Then she moved closer to him. "I kind of like it."

Not sure he'd heard her correctly, he turned slowly toward her. A nervousness not unlike that she'd displayed when she'd told him about Evan had her hugging herself and unable to hold his gaze for very long.

"That's scary for me to admit," she said.

"Why?"

She shrugged. "Probably something to do with my control issue."

"Maybe losing control isn't always a bad thing."

She raised her eyes and met his. "Maybe not."

"Mom!" Evan's voice invaded the moment, snatching Grace's attention away from Nathan.

"I've got to go," she said.

Before she could take a step, Nathan closed the distance between them and kissed her again. She clung to him and kissed him back with every bit as much enthusiasm. When they came apart, he thought he'd never seen such a thing of beauty.

"I don't know what's happening between us, but I like it."

She smiled. "I do, too." With that, she stepped away and hurried around the corner of the barn.

Nathan stood in the same spot for he wasn't sure how long, wondering how he could go from not even thinking about Grace to desiring every part of her in so few days. What kind of sense did that make?

Maybe it didn't have to make sense.

Grace rounded the edge of the barn with her heartbeat pounding against her eardrums.

"Hey, how were the kittens?" she asked.

"So cute!" Cheyenne said. "There's a little white one. I think they should name her Snowball."

The Farnsley boys rolled their eyes, and one of them made some sort of comment that Grace couldn't hear but that had Cheyenne giving them the evil eye.

"Why were you around the side of the barn?" Evan asked.

"Oh, nothing. Just looking out across the ranch, enjoying the view." Grace made the mistake of making eye contact with Laney, who cocked an eyebrow at her.

When Evan started that direction, Grace intercepted him and steered him toward their car. "Come on, stinky. We both need showers. We smell like horses and sweat."

Evan puffed his chest out. "It's manly."

"Well, your mother doesn't want to smell manly, so off we go."

The air went out of Evan's posturing and he headed toward the car. As Grace followed him, Laney fell into step beside her.

"That view wouldn't happen to be a 9.9 on the sexy scale, would it?"

"I don't know what you're talking about."

Laney laughed. "You better be glad interior design doesn't require the art of lying."

Grace kept walking.

"Come on, don't keep me in suspense. You're killing me here."

"What do you want to hear? That I've never been kissed like that in my life, that all I seem to be able to think about is Nathan and a distinct lack of clothing?"

Laney nodded and gave a wide grin of success. "Yeah, something like that."

"How do you weasel these things out of me?"

"Pure, unadulterated talent."

Grace rolled her eyes much like the Farnsley boys had moments ago.

Laney stepped closer and lowered her voice. "You've done more than kiss, haven't you? That's why you've been avoiding being alone with me all day."

Grace's cheeks flushed, causing Laney to squeal. "I knew it!"

"Shh! You don't have to broadcast it for all of Texas to hear."

Laney made a lame attempt at looking contrite. "So, was it everything you'd imagined? Please tell me it was better than sex with his half-drunk, teenage self."

Grace gave up trying to keep anything to herself. "It was wonderful."

Laney fanned herself and glanced beyond Grace, toward where Nathan was no doubt standing. "I suddenly wish Steven was here."

Grace half laughed, half snorted.

"So, tell me what happened."

As they walked slowly toward the parking area, Grace gave her the rundown of events from the kiss on the cabin porch to the one just now beside the barn.

"This sounds really good, Grace."

Grace stopped. "Part of me knows it's crazy to start anything with Nathan, but my willpower has flown the coop."

"Is that a bad thing?"

A mere few days ago, her immediate response would have been an unqualified yes. "I honestly don't know." She made a flippy motion toward her temple. "My head is all mixed up."

"Hmm, sounds like a woman falling in love to me."

Grace sighed, glanced over her shoulder toward the barn. "I wonder if I ever fell out of love with him."

Laney linked her arm with Grace's. "I think you and I have a long evening of chatting ahead of us. But like you, I reek of livestock. Meet you on the porch with a cold glass of lemonade in an hour?"

Grace thought for a second, then nodded. "That actually sounds really nice."

A little less than an hour later, Grace stepped out of her cabin and noticed Evan playing with the rest of the campers on the playground equipment that sat in the middle of the circle of cabins. She spotted Barrett at the same moment he saw her, too late to duck back inside the cabin.

"Hey, there. You look refreshed," he said as he walked toward her.

"Yeah. Was a long day."

"I'm hoping you still have enough energy left for dinner. I saw a nice steak place in town."

She hated to shoot him down, but she couldn't let him think there was any chance with her, either. Wise or not, her heart was already in the hands of another.

"Actually, Laney and I are having a relaxing girls' night. We're both pretty wiped after today."

Barrett nodded slowly, as though he got that she wasn't interested but appreciated the gentle brush off. He reached in his pocket and pulled out a card, extended it toward her. "Well, if you ever find yourself in Oklahoma City and in need of a dinner companion, give me a call."

Grace took the card and smiled at him. "It was nice getting to know you this week. I hope you had a good time with your boys."

"I did." He hesitated a moment, looking as if he wanted to say something else, then nodded before heading back toward his own cabin.

Grace shoved the card in the pocket of her capri pants and headed toward Laney's cabin. When she noticed her friend sitting there sipping lemonade, she wondered at what point she'd come outside.

"Truly, it must be such a burden having so many men vying for your affections," Laney said as Grace climbed the steps.

"Anyone ever tell you that you're evil?" Grace grabbed the other glass and took a long drink of lemonade before she sank into a chair.

"All the time." Laney smiled wide, pleased with herself.

"Barrett's a nice guy, but I'm just not the way he should be looking."

"Because you already have your sights set on another hot cowboy."

Grace leaned her head back against the chair. "Yeah."

"And you're regretting that?"

"Yes, and no."

"I see your powers of decisiveness are operating at full power."

Grace rolled her head sideways to look at Laney. "Talking to you really is exhausting sometimes. Tell me again why we're such good friends."

"My magnetic personality?"

Grace laughed. "Maybe because you're so shy and retiring."

This time, Laney laughed. They both watched as the kids climbed all over the monkey bars.

"How serious is it?" Laney asked. "Just having some hot sex, or are we talking lasting relationship here?"

"I don't know. I mean, I ran through so many scenarios in my head that I thought might happen when I came here and told him about Evan, but this wasn't even on the radar."

"Do you love him?"

Grace let herself really consider that question. Did she love him, or was it some residual infatuation from long ago? "Yes."

"Do you think he loves you?"

"He...well, he at the very least desires me."

"Sounds to me like you need to find out if what you're feeling is reciprocated before you can make any decisions."

Would Nathan loving her make things easier or more difficult? And did she really want to know the answer to that question?

Chapter Thirteen

Overall, their first Cowboy Camp for Kids had gone well. Some of the participants had already expressed interest in attending again if the Teagues hosted another. Though that was all great for the ranch's reputation and bottom line, Nathan couldn't wait to get those people out of there so he could spend more time with Grace and Evan. So he could find a way to convince Grace to stay beyond the few extra days she'd agreed to.

But first things first.

"I'd like to thank all of you for taking part in our first camp of this type. We've come to the time several of you have been waiting for—the announcement of the Cowboy Camper of the Week." The Farnsley boys looked confident, a couple of kids looked like they didn't care, Cheyenne was on the verge of jumping out of her little pink boots, and Evan…well, he looked so hopeful that for a moment Nathan considered he'd made a mistake. "Congratulations to Cheyenne Stuart."

Cheyenne squealed and ran forward. Nathan handed her the cowboy statue and shook her little hand. For a flash, he wondered what it would be like to have a daughter of his own. He glanced at Grace and found her consoling Evan.

By the time he'd shaken a lot of hands and shared a few last goodbyes with the campers and their parents, Evan had disappeared. Grace sat on the bench where she'd been sitting when she'd told him he was a father, talking to Cheyenne's mom. Over the past couple of days, he'd finally figured out that those two had been friends before arriving at the ranch. That explained the assessing looks Laney Stuart had cast his direction during the past week.

When Laney saw him now, she said a final word to Grace then headed down the hill to her car where Cheyenne stood admiring her award.

"Where's Evan?" he asked as he sauntered toward Grace.

"In the barn with the kittens. He said he wanted to say goodbye."

Fear shot through him. Had she changed her mind about staying?

"I haven't told him yet that we're staying a few extra days."

"Why not?"

She looked up at him. "In case I started listening to the voices in my head that are saying I'm just prolonging the inevitable."

It didn't have to be inevitable, but he couldn't talk to her about that at the moment. Right now, he needed to comfort his son.

He found Evan sitting in a bed of hay, running his fingertip gently over a tiny orange kitten.

"They're cute, aren't they?"

Evan looked at Nathan, his chin quivering. "Yeah." He quickly returned his attention to the kittens.

"I'm sorry you're upset about the award," Nathan said.

"It's okay." The sadness in Evan's voice said otherwise.

"You did great, but I thought maybe Cheyenne could get the award because you're getting something better."

Evan's forehead scrunched in confusion as he looked at Nathan. "What?"

"Your mom said you could stay on the ranch a few more days."

Evan's eyes widened. "Really?" He sounded as if Nathan had announced he was going to be able to go to the moon.

"Really."

Evan launched himself at Nathan and hugged him, hard. Unprepared, it took Nathan a moment to absorb the shock and then, slowly, wrap his arms around his son.

Something deep and visceral spoke aloud in his mind, telling him that he couldn't let Evan go. He had to convince Grace that now was the right time to tell Evan the truth, because he didn't even want to think about what Simon had suggested. He'd hurt Grace once before and didn't want to do it again.

But Evan would know Nathan was his father.

"You're sure you don't want me to stay?" Laney asked as Grace came down the hill to stand next to her.

"Yeah. You need to get back to work and

Cheyenne back to school. I appreciate you being here this week. Not sure I could have done it without knowing you were there if I needed you."

"Well, I might not be a cowboy freak like the rest of you, but it had its moments."

Grace smiled. "I don't know. I think maybe you have a bit of a cowgirl in you and you just don't want to admit it."

Laney laughed. "Did you fall off a horse onto your head?"

Grace glanced toward the barn, forcefully keeping herself from hurrying inside to see what Nathan was saying to Evan.

Laney grabbed her hand and squeezed. "I know I've teased you a lot this week, but I hope I didn't push you too much. That's a bad habit of mine."

Grace shook her head. "You didn't push me in any direction I wasn't already going."

"I hope everything works out, whatever you decide. And if you need me, don't hesitate to call. We will turn around and come right back."

Grace smiled, touched once again by how giving her friends were. Despite everything she'd gone through, she was a lucky woman. "Thank you, but I think I need to go forward on my own now."

"Okay." Laney lifted her index finger and pointed at Grace. "But I want you to call me and give me updates."

"Yes, ma'am." Grace leaned forward and gave Laney a hug. "Thanks again. I owe you."

Laney laughed and hugged Grace back then pulled away. "You can pay me back by coming to visit this summer. We'll do things that have nothing to do with smelly livestock and Wrangler jeans—like go to the spa."

"It's a deal." Grace leaned down to give Cheyenne a hug, too. "Try to keep your mom out of trouble, okay?"

Cheyenne nodded. "Okay." She said that single word in a way that made it sound as though it would be quite an undertaking, making Grace laugh.

"That's it. I'm being ganged up on, time to go," Laney said and opened her car door.

Grace watched as they slipped into the rental car and headed down the ranch road. She waved a final time as they rounded the curve that took them out of sight. Slowly, she turned toward the barn, but didn't head that direction. Instead, she returned to the bench and stared out across the pasture, trying to convince herself that she could get through the next few days. That the right path for the future would reveal itself to her so she could walk forward with confidence instead of second-guessing every thought that entered her head.

Part of Grace knew she was playing a dangerous game with her heart. The more time she spent with Nathan, the more he kissed her and made her feel as though he truly cared about her, the harder it was going to be to leave. Still, knowing that, she couldn't stop.

During the days that followed the departure of the rest of the campers, they sat together in the dark and kissed after Evan went to sleep. One day, Nathan surprised her by bringing her lunch from the Primrose when she was working at Merline's gallery. They'd sat on the floor, looking out at the lake, and fed each other. They took Evan to a movie, and she'd felt so much like they were a real family that she'd battled tears throughout the entire hour and a half. She'd begun to think maybe it was possible, if only she could be sure that Nathan felt as much for her as she did for him.

She could ask him straight out, but there was enough of her unsure, suspicious self left that she worried he'd say yes just to keep Evan close.

"You seem deep in thought."

Grace jumped at the sound of Nathan's voice so close to her ear. "Way to sneak up on a girl."

Nathan smiled, and it could only be called deliciously wicked. "Were you thinking about me?"

Yes.

"Only if you are lighting fixtures." She turned back to her work on the desk that had been delivered to the gallery that morning. "The installers are supposed to be here at two."

Nathan moved close behind her and nuzzled her neck. "An entire hour. What will we do with the time?"

She tried to move out of his grasp, though she wasn't particularly insistent about it. The man had only to touch her and all her natural resistance dissolved.

"I have work to do."

He stalked her around the small room, like a panther after prey. When she bumped up against the plush couch in the corner, he reached out and slid his hands along her jaw to the back of her head.

"There's time enough for that later." He reached back to shut and lock the office door. Then he kissed her, long and deep.

The next thing Grace knew they were spread

along the couch, shoving at each other's clothes. "Nathan, someone could walk in the building."

"I know."

She gasped as his mouth captured hers again. Never would she have thought it of herself, but the chance of discovery sent a thrill surging through her. It felt wicked, but she went with it and they were naked in short order. When Nathan entered her, she moaned his name, which seemed to light a fire in him. She dug her fingers into his back as they made very fast, panting love to one another.

Nathan's pace increased with each stroke, and her muscles tensed as her pleasure built. Her breath came faster and faster until she bowed upward as Nathan cried out in release.

"Keep going," she said. "Don't stop."

He did just that, taking her closer and closer and closer.

For the first time in her life, she didn't hold back. She met each thrust and when her release came, her cry sounded primal.

As the sound died away, embarrassment rushed in and Grace covered her face with her hands. "Oh, my goodness, I can't believe I acted like that. I've gone crazy."

Nathan shifted next to her and guided her

hands downward. "Don't. It was beautiful. You're beautiful."

She shook her head. "I've never done anything like that."

He smiled in that hard-to-resist way of his. "I'm happy to know I'm the one to make you lose control."

She examined his face, trying to read what he was thinking. "Nathan, what's going on here?"

"I thought that was obvious."

"Beyond that."

"We're having a good time together, Grace."

How could she expect words of love from him when they really barely knew each other? He didn't harbor old feelings that had been rekindled.

She managed a smile. "We are." She glanced at the clock on the wall. "But we'd better put on our clothes before the electrician crew gets here." She shifted off the couch, turning her back to him so she wasn't tempted to tell him how very much she loved him. Always had.

Probably always would.

Nathan lifted his hand to touch Grace's back, but something told him to stop, that it would somehow make things worse. How had they gone from the best sex he'd ever had to her visibly shutting down, closing invisible doors around herself? She still didn't trust him, not fully, and that hurt. What more could he do to convince her that he didn't have ulterior motives?

He had no answers, so he dressed and watched as she rounded the desk and started shifting through papers.

"Grace, I—"

The front door opened, drawing her attention. "The installers are here. I'll talk to you later." She nearly ran from the office without meeting his eyes.

Nathan stood in the middle of the office feeling as though the bottom of the world had fallen out from beneath him.

As the lighting guys spent the entire afternoon installing low-light fixtures, it was all Grace could do not to pace and scream. Why had she let herself get involved with Nathan? Why hadn't she just stuck with her original plan?

Because no matter how hard she tried to deny it, she wanted to be with Nathan...forever. But how was that possible if he didn't love her?

"That's it," said the head of the installation crew.

She examined their work and nodded. "Looks

wonderful. I appreciate you all coming out so quickly."

"We're grateful for the work."

She signed the necessary forms, shook the man's hand and watched the crew drive away. Then she wandered around the gallery, half marveling at how much she and Merline had gotten done in a few short days and half wondering what was the right move regarding Nathan. Should she just go home and try to put memories of him away as she'd done before? Maybe the right path was telling Evan the truth, letting him and his father have a relationship and seeing where hers with Nathan led, if anywhere.

Or maybe she should just tell Nathan the truth, that she loved him, and base her final decision on his reaction.

She grabbed her purse and headed out the door before she lost her nerve. No matter what happened, at least this time when she left Blue Falls, nothing would be left unsaid.

As she rounded the corner onto the end of Main Street, she braked to avoid a truck pulling out from the farm supply store. That's when she noticed Nathan standing on the opposite side of the street talking to a man in a suit. She watched as they shook hands and Nathan headed down the sidewalk. A glance back at the man revealed he was climbing a set of steps into a brick building.

Her heartbeat faltered when she spotted the writing on the front window: Adrian Stone, Attorney at Law.

Someone behind her honked, and she hit the gas while she tried to calm her pulse. There were any number of reasons Nathan might be talking to a lawyer. After all, his family owned a sizable ranching operation, and she imagined that came with legal concerns. Maybe they were just friends bumping into each other on the street.

No matter how much common sense she threw at herself on the drive back to the ranch, the need to get away from Blue Falls kept trumping them all. She wasn't going to lose her son—no matter if that loss came about because of a legal fight or her son's shifting alliances. She'd achieved the goal of the trip, so it was time to go.

She drove straight to the cabin. Best to pack everything before picking up Evan. She wasn't a fool and was well aware that Evan would most likely cry, especially after she'd told him they wouldn't be leaving until tomorrow. She needed to be back on her home turf where she felt stronger and more able to deal with whatever problems came her way, not off-kilter the way she'd been since returning to Blue Falls.

Her hands shook as she tossed their clothes and toiletries into the suitcases. Once she had them filled, she stowed them in the car.

The front door banged open. "Hey, Mom, guess what!" Evan's last word tapered off as he spotted the final bag in her hand.

Grace quickly tried to map out damage control in her head.

"You're packing already?" Evan asked.

"Uh, yes. We're actually leaving now. I have to get back to work."

"But your meeting isn't until Friday."

She took a few steps forward but halted when Evan backed away from her. "I have a lot of work to do, honey."

"You promised we could stay until tomorrow. I don't want to leave."

"Now don't argue, Evan. We've already stayed longer than I'd planned when we came here."

"No! I don't want to go back, not ever!" He rushed out the door, leaving it wide open behind him.

Grace choked on a sob but went after him. "Evan, come back here."

He ran around the edge of the cabin and

started down the path that led from the cabins toward the main part of the ranch. God, she'd made such a mistake by coming here. This wasn't her son, not this defiant boy. As she came around the corner of the cabin and made an awkward step off the end of the porch, dizziness swamped her and she put out a hand. Only nothing was there. Her breath came too fast.

Someone caught her, keeping her from collapsing as she watched her son grow tinier by the moment.

"Come on, sit down before you fall."

She looked at her rescuer and was surprised to see Hank. He guided her to the picnic table where she'd kissed Nathan.

"No, I have to get Evan."

Hank pressed gently but firmly on her shoulder until she sat. "He's going no farther than that barn. And it's my experience that when the boys get like this, it's better to just give them time to cool off before you try to talk to them."

"You don't understand. Evan doesn't act like this."

"Maybe he hasn't before, but he is now." Hank sank onto the bench beside her.

She pushed her palm back over the top of her head. "This was a bad idea."

"No, it wasn't."

Hank Teague was a man of few words, but in that moment Grace felt as if he saw and understood everything.

"Why do you say that?"

"Because a boy needs both parents."

She shook her head. "It's not that simple."

"And sometimes the parents need each other, whether they realize it or not."

Grace took a slow, deep breath, trying to stop the spinning in her head, her erratic pulse. The stabbing pain she'd felt when she'd seen Nathan with that attorney. All her fears that he'd been using her to get to Evan came roaring back. Still, she couldn't say all that. Couldn't risk Hank calling Nathan before she could get Evan and leave the ranch. She needed distance and time to sort everything out, to consult her own attorney. To possibly tell Evan the truth on her own terms before Nathan decided to do it for her. She only hoped that Hank hadn't noticed her packing the car and already given Nathan a heads-up.

"I appreciate how you all have treated Evan while we've been here and how you've honored my request to not tell him about his paternity."

Hank was quiet for a moment and didn't make eye contact with her. "My boy loves you, you know?"

He couldn't have shocked her more if he'd announced he was the King of England. "No, I don't know."

"He's a lot like me. It took almost losing Merline to another man for me to say the words. I'd loved her for months, but I'd never told her. After I told her, she said she'd known all along. She just wasn't going to let me off easy without saying the words."

Grace stared down the hillside, desperate to escape before Nathan returned to the ranch. She didn't want to fall apart in front of him and couldn't stand the thought of Evan making a scene, casting her in a bad light in comparison to his new hero. She stood and started to leave.

"Sometimes actions speak louder than words," Hank said.

She stopped and looked at Evan's grandfather. Would Nathan look like that when he aged? Would Evan?

"And sometimes the words are more important than anything else."

Nathan didn't go back to the ranch immediately after talking with Adrian Stone. Instead, he got a cup of takeout coffee from the Primrose and went to sit by the lake. The final hours of Grace and Evan's extended stay were ticking away, and he couldn't tell if she was any closer to changing her mind about telling Evan the truth. He'd chosen the tactic of not pushing her, but he needed an answer tonight. He couldn't have them leaving with how things stood.

The fact was he didn't want them leaving at all. After being with Grace, he'd developed a need for her every bit as strong as that to get to know his son. The thought of her a day's drive away, where he couldn't kiss her or make love to her, didn't sit well.

Was he falling in love with her? Had he already fallen and was just too dumb to realize it? And if he told her that, would she believe him? What she'd endured in her past had left her with significant trust issues, and he couldn't honestly say he blamed her. But if what they'd shared the past few days hadn't begun to change her mind about him and that he wanted more than Evan, what would?

Maybe he should just ask her.

He chucked the empty coffee cup in the nearest trash can, walked back to his truck and made the drive back to the ranch determined not to take no for an answer. Before the sun rose again, he was determined that Evan would know who his father was and Grace Cameron would trust him enough to give life in Blue Falls another try.

He didn't drive up to the cabins first thing but rather to his own house to take a shower and change. Once he cleaned up, he headed for her cabin to find her car gone. Thinking she might be down at the main part of the ranch, he went there. No luck there, either. He should have checked at the gallery before leaving town but hadn't thought about it.

When he walked into the kitchen of his parents' house, he found his parents sitting at the dining room table with a couple of cups of coffee.

"Have you all see Grace?"

A meaningful look passed between his mom and dad, one that caused his gut to knot. His mom stood slowly and faced him.

"They're gone."

"Gone to town?" Please let it just be into Blue Falls.

Sadness tugged at his mother's face as she clutched the back of the dining room chair. "Back home."

"When? How long ago?"

"Couple of hours."

Nathan headed for the door, determined to break every speed limit to catch her.

"Don't."

The single word from his father was so surprising that Nathan hesitated and turned to face him. "What?"

"You need to let her go."

"Why would I do that? She has my son and he doesn't even know it. She ran out of here like a thief."

"Because you care about her."

"I thought I did." Nathan retraced his steps and gripped the edge of the kitchen island so hard he thought he might crush the granite. "Why would she leave like that? I thought things were going well."

"Something had her pretty spooked."

Nathan eyed his father. "You saw her? Why didn't you stop her?"

"I didn't know she was leaving at the time. Evan was upset, she was upset. So we talked a little bit, hoping the boy would calm down." His dad paused, fiddled with the handle of his cup. "And it wasn't my place to change her mind even if I had known."

Nathan pushed away from the island and threw his hands up. "Then you all don't care that your only grandchild has no idea you're his grandparents? That he'll go on living in the dark, in another state, if Grace has her way?"

His mom came to stand beside him. "Of course we care. We want Grace and Evan here as much as you do."

"Then why didn't you call me as soon as you discovered she'd left?"

"What are you going to do, Nathan? Pull her over and have an argument on the side of the highway?"

"If I have to."

"How likely do you think she'll be to change her mind if you accost her like that?"

"Well, being nice certainly didn't do the trick."

His mom tried to move closer, but he backed away.

"What did you want her to do? Leave her entire life behind, everything she's built for herself and Evan?"

"They could have a good life here, too. Evan likes the ranch, and he's young enough to start over making new friends."

"But what about Grace?"

"People have houses here that probably need decorating."

"I don't think that's the top thing on her mind."

"Then what the hell is, because for the life of me I don't know what that woman wants."

He met his mother's eyes and saw knowledge there, that ability she had to read people so well.

"She wants you, Nathan. And I think, deep down, you know that she loves you. The question is, do you love her?"

All his fight fell away as the truth finally slid home in his heart. "Yes, I love her."

His mom smiled. "Then that's what you need to tell her."

Chapter Fourteen

Despite being back home and back to work, surrounded by all the things that were normal, Grace couldn't find any peace. Evan only spoke to her when he had to, remaining upset longer than she had anticipated. Even though she was happy that she and Emily had landed the lodge deal, she found it hard to concentrate. Ever since they'd left the ranch three weeks before, she'd slept terribly and was sick to her stomach more often than not. The truth was, she missed Nathan. And even though she'd been the one to run away, her heart ached that he hadn't called her. How crazy was that?

She'd lost count of how many times she'd

wondered how differently things might have turned out if she'd just taken a leap of faith and told Evan the truth. Maybe Nathan wouldn't have gone to that attorney and turned her life upside down again. And maybe she wouldn't have fled Blue Falls for a second time because of the hurt he'd caused.

But had he caused it, really? For several days, the idea that maybe he'd been there for another reason had been gnawing at her. She hadn't even asked, hadn't waited to find out. She'd done what she'd been prepared to do from the moment she'd stepped foot back on that ranch—run. And she didn't like herself much because of it.

Sometimes she wondered why, if Nathan supposedly cared so much about Evan, he hadn't tried to contact her. With each passing day with no word, she expected to hear from that attorney. But it was as if she and Evan had never gone to Texas. Except, of course, for how Evan avoided her now.

And the hole that had reopened in her heart after leaving Nathan behind again.

She'd been a fool, in so many ways.

"How long is this going to go on?"

Grace looked up to see Emily standing in the doorway to her office, leaning against the door frame with her arms crossed. That's when she realized she'd drifted off into her thoughts again, leaving the sketch in front of her half-drawn.

"I'm sorry."

"You don't have to be sorry. I'm just worried about you."

She started to instinctually say she was fine, but she couldn't force out those words anymore. "I feel lost, Em, like all of my insides have been ripped out and only part of them returned. And the problem is, I don't know how to fix it. It might be too late to fix it."

"He still hasn't called?"

"No. And at this point I think it's safe to say he's not going to."

Emily came fully into the room and sank into the chair opposite Grace's drawing table. "Then maybe you should call him. I think it's the only thing that's going to let you move on, to find out what his plans are, how he feels about you."

"Honestly, do you think he could have any affection for me after what I did? Again. From his point of view, I've screwed him over twice. And he's right."

"You know I'll support you whatever you decide, but you've got to do something. You can't keep going on the way you have been. I think I've seen you eat exactly three crackers and an apple since you've been back, you look like you haven't slept in a month, and your concentration got left somewhere not here."

Grace doodled at the edge of the paper in front of her. "I've got to tell Evan the truth and hope he doesn't hate me for not telling him sooner. I can't stand how things are between us now. It's like I've already lost him."

"Maybe if you let Nathan be a part of his life, things will actually be better."

Grace wasn't so sure, but then she wasn't sure about anything anymore.

The front door opened, and Grace started to slide from her chair.

"I'll handle it," Emily said as she stood and headed toward the reception area.

Grace was looking at the sketch, trying to focus on the right kind of window treatments for the lodge's guest rooms, when Emily reappeared in the doorway, a stunned expression on her face.

"What's wrong?"

"Nathan's here."

Grace's heartbeat stumbled and she dropped the pencil she was holding. Nathan, here? All the ways she'd imagined starting another conversation with him crashed into each other like a fifty-car pileup in her head. Her legs shook as she stood, and for a moment she thought they were going to dump her on the floor. Her head swam but she managed to blink a few times to focus and steady herself. But before she could walk toward the door, there he was, standing behind Emily.

"You okay?" Emily asked her even though she had to know Nathan was right there.

Grace nodded and Emily reluctantly moved away with a final glance between her and Nathan. Guilt and shame swamped Grace, but she forced herself to maintain eye contact with Nathan as he stepped into her office, his hat in his hands.

"Hello, Nathan."

"Grace."

She could have offered him a seat, a drink, and they could have danced around what he'd no doubt come here to discuss, but she didn't think she could take it.

"I'm going to tell him, tonight."

Nathan looked startled by her direct approach, but she didn't give him a chance to speak. She had to get this out before she chickened out.

"I'd already decided before I saw you. I'm

going to risk having him hate me because I can't stand the thought of going through a custody battle. He doesn't deserve to be used as a rope in a tug of war."

"Grace—"

She held up a hand. "No, let me finish. I'm sorry I left without telling you why. I just hope you won't hold it against me. If it makes you feel any better, Evan didn't want to leave and he barely talks to me now."

"How could that possibly make me feel better?" he asked, ignoring her plea to let her speak uninterrupted.

"Maybe you think that it's my due for how I've treated you."

"I hope you don't really think I'm that cruel."

"I..." Words refused to come. It was as if her brain had fizzled, and she couldn't grasp a single coherent thought. She sank back onto her chair before she collapsed.

"Why did you leave like that?"

She lowered her gaze, ashamed of how she'd acted on impulse instead of solid facts. "I saw you talking with that attorney in town, and all my old fears came roaring back to life. I just knew you were going to try to take Evan away from me." She shook her head. "I know

I sound crazy when I say it out loud. Maybe I am a little crazy."

"You're not crazy. I did go see him to find out what my rights as a father are."

"Oh." Her nerves stretched to near the breaking point.

"I had to, Grace. I wasn't sure if you'd ever tell Evan, but he's my son. I have a right to see him."

"I know." Grace's voice came out weak, mirroring how she felt.

"But that's not the only reason I was there. I also asked Adrian what I needed to do to leave my share of the ranch to Evan in my will."

She looked up so fast that her head swam again.

"When you came to the ranch, you were looking out for Evan's future. It was my turn."

"Oh, Nathan." Tears pooled in her eyes. "I'm so sorry. I… I thought when I didn't hear anything from you or the attorney that maybe…" She couldn't finish, and he must have sensed it because he stepped forward and lifted her hands in his.

"It took me this long to cool off and see things clearly. I know it's hard for you to trust people, but I'm asking you to trust me."

She forced herself to meet his gaze. "Where do we go now?"

"We tell Evan, together, then go from there."

She nodded though her insides were roiling like a hurricane. A glance at the clock told her it was later than she expected. "He should be here any minute. He rides the bus here after school."

The light of anticipation in Nathan's eyes told her all she needed to know about how he felt toward his son. If something happened to her, Evan would be okay.

When she heard the front door open followed by the sound of Evan's small footfalls, Grace stood. "That's him." She made her way shakily to the reception area where she noticed Emily hadn't retreated all the way to her office.

She offered Emily a small smile then turned toward her son. "Evan, someone is here to see you."

He looked up slowly from a handheld gaming system, like the Farnsley boys had had—a guilt gift she'd given him in hopes he'd start speaking to her again. It hadn't worked. Instead, he used it to avoid her even more, and she'd not had the strength or heart to take that from him, too. She knew what a broken heart felt like and how long it took to get over one and move on.

She knew the moment Nathan stepped out of her office because Evan's face transformed to sheer joy. As he raced past her toward Nathan, she closed her eyes and prayed for the strength to get through what was to come.

Having Evan stick close by his side, asking to ride with him back to Grace's house and hanging on his every word, felt so good, as if Nathan was some sort of conquering hero. Wasn't that the way little boys were supposed to look at their fathers? He knew he had at Evan's age.

But as they arrived at Grace's and went inside, as she set about cooking an early dinner, he saw how much their son's reaction cost her. That more than anything else was what told him how bad things had been since she'd left the ranch.

"Kiddo, what do you say we help your mom fix dinner?"

Grace glanced over her shoulder where she stood at the kitchen counter cutting up vegetables. "I'm fine, thanks." Her voice sounded exhausted, the same as how she looked. As soon as they finished the big conversation with

Evan, he was getting her alone and making sure she was okay. He didn't like the look of those dark circles under her eyes and the way she moved as if she was barely staying upright.

He ignored her insistence that she could handle everything on her own and went to stand next to her. From this moment forward, he'd do whatever he had to do to convince her she wouldn't have to face anything on her own ever again. She turned her suspiciously bright eyes up toward him. He placed his hand over the top of hers.

"Tell me what to do."

She relented. "You can finish chopping these. Evan, get the big salad bowl."

Evan moved to do as he was told, and Nathan didn't miss how she looked at the boy with surprise.

"He's been difficult lately?" he asked low where Evan couldn't hear him.

Grace sighed. "He didn't want to leave the ranch, or you." She tried to smile, but she couldn't quite pull it off. "Turns out you weren't the reason I lost him. I did that all by myself."

"Grace." He tried to comfort her, but she moved toward the refrigerator. It hurt to watch her in pain, and he hoped that by the end of tonight everything would be in the open and Evan would accept him and stop being cold to his mother.

As they sat down to dinner several minutes later, Nathan kept up a running conversation with Evan but his gaze insisted on drifting to Grace. He wanted so much to pull her into his arms and tell her that he loved her, that she didn't have to be sad or scared anymore. But they needed to get the necessary conversation with Evan over with so she'd at least stop dreading that.

"Why'd you come to see us, Nathan?" Evan asked as Nathan was watching Grace move a bite of salmon around on her plate with her fork. Her eyes lifted to his and there was knowledge and acceptance there that the time had come.

Nathan returned his attention to his son. "Well, your mom and I have something we need to talk to you about."

Evan shifted his eyes between Nathan and Grace.

Grace slid her hand across the table and wrapped it around one of Evan's smaller ones. Nathan was glad to see the boy didn't pull away.

"You know how I've always said that your

father lived somewhere else, that maybe you'd get to meet him someday?"

Evan nodded.

"Well, Nathan is your father."

Evan's eyes went wide. "Really?"

Grace nodded. "Yes, really."

"That's awesome!" Evan slid from his seat and ran around the table to hug Nathan.

Nathan's heart flipped at the gesture, but when he looked at Grace, she was biting her bottom lip and tears were very close to spilling down her cheeks. He clasped one of her hands to reassure her. She gave a little squeeze back then stood and started clearing the table.

"Does that mean I get to live at the ranch?" Evan asked.

Nathan was still watching Grace so he saw her slip the moment Evan asked that question. He shot to his feet and got to her just before she hit the floor. His heart slammed against his ribcage as he watched her eyes roll back in her head.

Evan fell to his knees beside her. "Mom! Mom!" Evan shook her, trying to get her to wake up. The fear in his voice ripped at Nathan, telling him just how scary it must have been for Evan to watch his mother's battle against cancer.

Pure, potent fear of his own, like nothing he'd ever felt, seared every part of Nathan. "Come on, Grace, wake up. Evan, call 9-1-1."

Evan hesitated for a moment, as though he was afraid to leave his mother's side. Nathan squeezed the boy's shoulder, forcing him to look at him. "It's okay, son. I'll stay with her."

Evan hopped up and raced for the phone. When Nathan returned his attention to Grace, she stirred and her eyes opened partway though they remained unfocused.

God, please let her be okay. I'll do whatever she wants. Just let her be okay.

For a short moment, her eyes focused on him. "Take care of Evan."

Fear shot through him at the tinge of finality in her words. Before he could respond, she went back under.

Grace awoke to a familiar but hated beeping. The antiseptic smell of a hospital made her nose twitch. She slowly opened her eyes, expecting a harsh glare but finding the room only dimly lit. And Nathan asleep at an uncomfortable angle in the chair next to her bed. Pieces of the moments before she collapsed started coalescing in her mind. Her revealing the truth to Evan. His joy at the news, then his question about living at the ranch. The way the world had spun around her. Nathan calling her name before she faded into oblivion.

She bit her lip as tears pooled in her eyes. Evan knew the truth, knew she'd hidden it from him. He'd already wanted to stay at the ranch. How much more must he want to stay with his newly discovered father now?

Nathan grunted and shifted in the chair. She stared at him and noticed how furrowed his brow was, as if he was having a nightmare. Just as she was about to reach out and touch him, a nurse walked in the door. Grace jerked her hand back to her side.

"Oh, good, you're awake. You gave a lot of people a scare," the petite blonde said quietly with a glance at Nathan.

"What's wrong with me?"

"Dehydrated for one. The doctor will be here in the morning to talk with you."

"What time is it?"

"A little after 2:00 a.m." She nodded toward Nathan as she checked Grace's vitals. "And this one hasn't left your side since they brought you in."

He hadn't? Her heart sped up at that, and the nurse gave her a knowing smile before making a note in her chart then leaving the room.

Nathan shifted again then opened his eyes. It took him a moment to focus on her. When he did, he jerked upright.

"Grace! You're awake."

He looked so worried. She wasn't sure why that surprised her, but it did.

"Just for a few minutes."

"How do you feel? Do you need anything?"

"Some answers." She hadn't meant to say it aloud, but it was out there now. Best to get everything done and not procrastinate, right?

He sat up straighter. "Okay."

"Where is Evan?"

"At Emily's. He refused to leave, so she had to wait until he fell asleep."

She grasped his hand where it rested on the side of the bed. "You must think I'm irrevocably broken."

"No. Just tired, stressed. Having to do too much on your own. Well, that stops right now."

"What do you mean?"

"I love you."

Grace froze, afraid her deepest desire had manufactured the words she most wanted to hear.

"You heard me right," Nathan said as he shifted from the chair to the edge of the bed. "I love you, Grace Cameron, and I want you and

Evan to come back to the ranch because I don't plan to live another day without you next to me. And while I'll move to Arkansas if I have to, Texas is in my blood and Evan would have deep roots there. I know I'd be asking you to give up a lot, and that's not fair, but you could start a good business in Blue Falls, maybe in the extra space at the gallery. I—"

"Nathan."

"Yes?"

"Say it again."

That slow, sexy smile transformed his face. "I love you."

"I love you, too." She took his hand between hers and held it next to her heart. "I think I always have."

Grace watched the minutes tick by the next morning, anxiety building exponentially with each one. She needed to know why she'd fainted, had to be sure the cancer hadn't returned just as she'd found the ultimate happiness. Could fate be so cruel? Hadn't she paid enough?

She glanced toward where Nathan stood looking out the window.

He'd said the words. She believed them.

And that changed absolutely everything.

She'd convinced him to go back to her house for a few hours only by teasing him that he needed a shower. She'd threatened to not talk to him again until he'd gotten some sleep in an actual bed. He'd gone but been back in time to accompany her breakfast tray into the room.

Voices outside the room drew her attention. Dr. Hamilton, her personal physician, walked in accompanied by the nurse who'd been in to check on her right after the shift change that morning.

The doctor extended his hand. "Good morning, Grace."

Grace shook his hand. "Hello."

Nathan came to sit beside her and clasped her hand, lending support. He knew why she was worried. They'd talked about a possible recurrence of her cancer into the wee hours. Remembering his words gave her a needed boost of strength.

We'll deal with whatever it is together. I'm not letting anything take you away from me.

"We got your test results back this morning," Dr. Hamilton said. "Nothing of any true concern there."

Grace couldn't let go of her fear quite yet. "The cancer—it hasn't come back?"

"No, still clear. It looks like you were dehydrated. Sometimes stress can affect our bodies like this, a warning sign to try to chill out. Oh, and you're pregnant."

She couldn't have heard him correctly. "What?"

"Barely, less than a month, but you are pregnant. So, drink plenty of fluids and come see me next week." He smiled and patted her hand. "We'll get you discharged soon."

Grace couldn't process the doctor's words as any kind of truth. She simply sat and stared at his retreating back until Nathan started laughing.

"Why in the world are you laughing?"

"Oh, no reason. Just the fact that I must be really virile because every time I make love to you, you get pregnant. We must be meant to be together."

She swatted him, outwardly scolding while inside the happiness swelled. She was going to have another child, and with Nathan, the man she loved with all her heart, body and soul. "That's not a reason to be together."

He captured her hand and kissed her fingers. "Is my being madly in love with you reason enough?"

Tears pooled in her eyes, an overflow of emotion she wasn't big enough to contain.

Nathan nodded toward her. "Happy tears?"

"Definitely."

"Good." He reached into his pocket and pulled something out. "Because I have something very important to ask you." He opened his hand, and a wooden ring with carved, painted wildflowers lay on his palm. "During those weeks after you left, I had Ryan make this for me because I want you and Evan, and now this new baby, to be my family." He lifted her hand and caressed her ring finger. "Will you marry me, Grace Cameron?"

She bit her trembling lip and could barely see through the tears, but she nodded. "Yes."

Evan surprised her by rushing into the room and jumping onto her bed. He gave her a huge hug, which she returned with a bursting joy in her heart to have him back.

"Does this mean I can call Nathan 'Dad'?"

Grace noticed the look of stunned wonder on Nathan's face, and she couldn't imagine how she'd ever doubted the man before her. She caressed the top of Evan's head. "Yes, it does. And you know what else?"

"What?"

"You're going to be a big brother."

It took a couple of beats for her meaning to sink in. When it did, Evan lifted to his knees on the mattress, pumped his fist, and said, “That’s awesome!”

Nathan met her gaze with what could only be love shining in his. “Yes, it is.”

Epilogue

"You look beautiful," Emily said over Grace's shoulder as they both stood in front of the full-length mirror.

Grace smiled as she ran her hand over the soft, flowing layers of silk organza. With her complexion, she didn't normally wear white, but today it was absolutely perfect.

Today, she would become Grace Teague.

"I feel like it's all a dream," she said.

Emily squeezed her shoulder as Laney stepped into view on the other side.

"More like a dream come true," Laney said.

Grace reached up and squeezed their hands where they lay on her shoulders. "Thank you."

"For what?" Emily asked.

"For being my best friends, for being there when I had no one else in the world."

Emily hugged her from behind. "You would have done the same for us. Now stop with the mushy before you make me cry. I don't want to do my makeup again." Emily stepped away, her bluebonnet-blue dress trailing after her.

Grace bit her bottom lip to keep from crying herself. Emily had been wonderful over the past month. When Grace had given her best friend the news that she was getting married and moving to Texas, Emily hadn't been upset. She'd been thrilled—not that Grace and Evan were moving away, but that they'd found the love and support of a family they both deserved. And in true Emily style, she'd cast the situation in a positive light, saying that Grace could just open a second office of Dynamic Duo Designs in Blue Falls.

Together, they'd gotten the Franklin Mountain Lodge project under way and worked out a plan in which they each could travel to help the other when big jobs demanded it.

And they'd bought a new copier that Emily had actually hugged on sight. The memory caused a wide grin to spread across Grace's face. If Emily could show that much love for a copy machine, how much more could she give a real live man?

"You do know that I have to play matchmaker for you now, right?" Grace said. "And I have an accomplice." She nodded toward Laney, who stood inside the adjoining bathroom putting the finishing touches on her upswept hairstyle.

"Goody, more matchmaking!" Laney clapped her hands.

"Oh, no, you don't." Emily shook her bouquet of white calla lilies. "I'm way too busy for a man, especially now that my partner is running off and leaving me."

"Hey!" Grace grabbed a pillow off the bed—Nathan's bed, soon to be her bed—and tossed it at Emily.

Her friend dodged it with a burst of laughter. Grace managed to hear a knock at the door over the commotion.

"Come in."

The door opened to reveal Merline, looking lovely in a mint-green dress that didn't have an ounce of mother-in-law frump in it anywhere. It suited her.

"Sounds like you all are having a good time in here."

Emily walked over and hooked her arm

around Merline's. "They're ganging up on me, Merline. They're in a matchmaking mood."

Merline looked thoughtful for a moment. "I do still have two available sons."

Emily rolled her eyes as Laney and Grace laughed.

"It's a conspiracy!" Emily said in dramatic fashion, eliciting more laughter from around the room. "I think I need a drink."

"Trudy can get you something in the kitchen," Merline said. Trudy, the ranch's long-time cook, was on the verge of retiring, but she'd insisted on staying to help with the wedding.

Some unspoken message seemed to pass between Merline and Grace's two bridesmaids because Laney and Emily made a quick exit. When the door closed behind them, Merline turned toward Grace and smiled.

"You are absolutely stunning."

"Thanks. You are, too."

Merline walked forward and took Grace's hands. "I am so happy for you and Nathan. And, honestly, I'm happy for me. Not only do I get grandchildren out of the deal, but I get the daughter I never had."

A lump rose in Grace's throat, and tears threatened. "I've never told anyone this, but all those years ago, when I was tutoring Nathan, I used to fantasize about you being my mom. You were so different than my mother—loving, fun and full of appreciation for life. Mom always seemed like life was a penance she had to pay or something."

Merline squeezed Grace's hands. "I think your family was unhappy and afraid to admit it. Somewhere along the way, they just fell victim to a warped sense of how things should be. But none of that is your fault. You deserve happiness and beauty because you bring that to others."

Grace bit her trembling lower lip.

"You officially become my daughter today, but you were already my daughter in my heart," Merline said.

Grace wrapped Merline in a tight hug. "Thank you," she whispered past the growing constriction in her throat.

Merline held her for several moments before stepping back. "I have something for you." She pulled a small white box out of her bag and handed it to Grace. "I don't know how much Nathan has told you about my family, but my mother raised my brother, sister and me alone. She worked a great deal to make ends meet, so I was shocked when she gave me this on my wedding day."

Grace's hands shook as she opened the box to reveal a string of pearls. "Oh, Merline, I can't take these from you. They hold too much meaning."

"No arguing. Passing them on to you is as it should be. You're a part of my family now. And maybe you'll have a daughter to give them to one day."

Grace thought about the child she carried, wondered if it might be a daughter. She imagined how wonderful Nathan would be with a little girl. He'd protect her with the ferocity of a lion and teach her to ride and appreciate the land that had been in her family for generations.

Merline took the necklace and stepped behind Grace to put it on her. The pearls felt cool and warm all at once, full of love and history.

"Now, I think it's time for you to make a very important walk. Your escort is waiting for you, and I must say he looks rather dashing."

Grace kissed Merline on the cheek then grabbed her bouquet of white lilies and bluebonnets. She followed Merline into Nathan's living room where Evan waited for her, dressed to the nines in a black suit and tie and shiny black shoes. He looked so much older it startled her.

"Mom, you're so pretty."

Those darn tears threatened again. "And you, sir, are very handsome."

A glance at Cheyenne, dressed in a pale blue dress and ready to do her part as flower girl, revealed that she seemed to agree by the look on her face.

"Well, let's get the show on the road," Emily said.

Grace couldn't agree more. She was more than ready to become Mrs. Nathan Teague.

After Merline left, they waited a couple of minutes then filed out of the house. Grace grasped Evan's hand as they headed down the flagstone path Nathan and his brothers had built over the past month leading from the house to that spectacular overlook. While everyone else would just appreciate the spot's beauty, for her and Nathan it held so much more meaning.

For today, Ryan had taken over Nathan's guitar, and he played the beautiful song Nathan had written for her, called simply "Grace." When Nathan had played it for her the night before, tears had flowed at the perfection of it. By strength of will, she didn't cry now.

As Evan guided her out of the woods, she caught sight of Nathan and her heart started racing, as if it was trying to reach him. He smiled, and she knew she'd never seen a more gorgeous sight.

As she and Evan reached Nathan, Evan tugged on her hand. She bent down to face her son.

"Are you happy, Mom?" he asked.

"Yes. Very, very happy."

"I'm glad." He kissed her cheek and went to take his spot next to Hank and Merline.

Grace only half heard the ceremony because all of her attention was focused firmly on Nathan and the love she saw in his eyes, a love that mirrored her own. She did manage to say "I do" at the appropriate spot, causing Nathan's smile to grow wider. Her heart sped up again when the minister said the words she'd been waiting for all day.

"By the power vested in me, I now pronounce you husband and wife. You may kiss the bride."

Nathan pulled her closer. "I love you, Mrs. Teague."

"I love you, Mr. Teague."

And she kissed him to prove it.

* * * * *